ACCORDING TO THE EVIDENCE

D1104900

ACCORDING TO THE EVIDENCE

by
HENRY CECIL

Published in 1988 by

Academy Chicago Publishers
425 North Michigan Avenue
Chicago, Illinois 60611

Library of Congress Cataloging-in-Publication Data

Cecil, Henry, 1902—
    According to the evidence.

    I. Title.
PR6053.E3A64   1988   823'.914   87-35170
ISBN 0-89733-295-4 (pbk.)

CHAPTER I

TRIAL FOR MURDER

THE prisoner had been to a public school, the charge was murder, the victim an attractive girl, and there had been several similar unsolved murders not long before. So, of course, the Cunningham Assize Court was crowded.

"Members of the jury," said counsel for the prosecution, "it is no part of my duty to emphasize to you the atrocious nature of this crime. On the contrary, I tell you that, as far as the prosecution is concerned, the only matter which you have to decide is whether the accused committed it or not. You must not let the natural horror which you no doubt feel at this deed influence you against the accused in the least. It cannot be disputed that someone killed this girl, it cannot be disputed that the man who killed her is a brute of the worst description; the sole question in issue between the prosecution and the defence is whether the prisoner is that brute. So, on behalf of the prosecution, I invite you, as far as possible, to put out of your minds the ghastly nature of the act and to forget that, if this man did murder this girl, he must be a fiend indeed. Consider only whether he is the man. I have to admit that, though it is easy for me to make such a submission to you, it may not be altogether easy for you to give effect to it, particularly in view of the injuries which were inflicted and the fact that the girl was of the highest character."

Counsel continued in the same strain for some minutes. He then outlined the substance of the evidence against the accused.

"On the fifth of December," he said, "at about six p.m., Ellen Wimslow left her home apparently to do a little shopping. Several people saw her in the town. She was last seen there in a café. A man was sitting at the same table. There is some evidence that it was the prisoner, but I do not stress this, as the waitress who thinks it was he is not absolutely certain about it. However, I shall call her and you must judge for yourselves. At about half-past seven a friend of Ellen's—Norah Parker—passed her walking across the common towards her home with a man. Ellen was never seen alive again. Her parents were not unduly alarmed at her not being home by half-past seven, but when eight o'clock came they became anxious. Ellen, as I have told you, was a girl of the highest character and she was also of a punctual nature. Her parents, fearing an accident, communicated with the police and the hospital. There had been no accident. At half-past eight Ellen's parents started to make inquiries among their neighbours, and as a result of what Norah Parker told them, they searched the common. Eventually, at about nine-fifteen, they found her—dead, with the injuries which I have described. The medical evidence will be that she must have been dead about an hour. There were traces of blood on her finger-nails; it was of the same group as that of the prisoner. But as that is the most common group the prosecution lays no stress on that factor. Had it been of a different group, it would have done much to prove the prisoner's innocence. As it is, the only conclusion I ask you to draw from the analysis of the blood on the finger-nails is that the murderer could have been the prisoner. But the blood did show that there must be a scratch or scratches on the murderer. On the body being discovered, the police made immediate inquiries and naturally they tried to find the man with whom Norah Parker had seen Ellen just before the murder had taken place. I do not think that it will be disputed that that man either committed the murder or, at the least, might be able to give information which could have assisted the police in their task. Accordingly, nation-wide appeals were made to him to come forward—in the Press, by radio, placards, and advertisements. No one answered the appeal. If the man was not the murderer, one wonders why. It is difficult to think that he did not hear or read the appeal. It received the widest publicity. Of course, if he was the murderer there was an excellent reason for not coming forward. In the course of their investigations Norah Parker was shown by the police a number of photographs and, with some hesitancy, she picked out one as being something like the man she had seen with Ellen. She will tell you that the photograph was of a younger man and she could not be at all sure that it was the same man, but of all the hundreds of photographs she looked at, it was the only one which she chose. Members of the jury, that photograph was a photograph of the prisoner."

Counsel paused to gain the necessary effect from what he had said and what he was about to say.

"And that photograph," he went on, "was taken ten years ago. At this stage I will only make this comment. If the prisoner was not the man, it is an extraordinarily unfortunate coincidence for him that Miss Parker should have picked out his photograph. As a result, within ten days of the murder, Chief Inspector Brooke went to see the prisoner who, as you will hear, lived in Medlicott—a town some fifty miles away from Greenly, where Ellen lived, but on the same railway line. You will hear from the inspector what took place at that interview. It is sufficient for me to tell you now three things: first, that the prisoner denied that he had ever been to Greenly on or about the day of the murder, and secondly—secondly, that there were two faint marks on the prisoner's face which might have been the remains of scratches. Thirdly, the prisoner told the inspector that he had scratched his face about ten days previously through brushing it against a branch of a tree in the dark in his garden. Members of the jury, if, when you have heard the whole evidence, you are satisfied that the prisoner was at Greenly on the night of the murder, that he was the man who was seen walking with Ellen, you may be equally satisfied that he is guilty of the crime with which he is charged. If he was innocent, why should he deny having been at Greenly? Perhaps my learned friend may suggest a reasonable answer. Or if you, members of the jury, can think of such an answer, by all means take it into consideration. I can only say that the prosecution is unable to suggest any. And then, members of the jury, what about the scratches? Another coincidence? If so, the prisoner is certainly a very unlucky man. By coincidence, Miss Parker picks out the wrong man and by coincidence that man had his face scratched at about the time of the murder. Shortly after his interview with the inspector, the prisoner was asked if he would have any objection to attending an identification parade. He said he had no objection. He stood among twenty people similarly dressed, of similar ages and of a condition in life similar to his. You will hear what took place at that parade. I need only tell you now that Miss Parker identified the prisoner. Another terrible coincidence, if the prisoner is innocent. But the coincidences do not stop there. The ticket collector at Greenly station will tell you that just before the last train left for Medlicott—you will remember that is where the prisoner lived—a man of the same build and type as the prisoner came hurriedly through the barrier. The collector cannot identify the prisoner. Indeed, you might feel doubtful of his evidence if he could, but he will tell you that he is quite satisfied that the two men—if there were two—were of the same type and that the man he saw wore a grey trilby hat. The prisoner had at home such a hat."

And so counsel went on, building up the case against the prisoner and effectively calling the attention of the jury to the way in which the coincidences were increasing in number if the prisoner were innocent. At last he finished and called his evidence. The most important witness was, of course, Norah Parker. She was an educated girl who gave her evidence quietly and well, though she felt extremely nervous. The pageantry and solemnity at an Assize Court are sufficient in themselves to make a witness nervous, but the knowledge that her evidence might be responsible for sending a man to his death naturally increased Miss Parker's nervousness. In spite of this, she controlled herself remarkably well. It is indeed astonishing how many witnesses, who are wholly unused to giving evidence, are able to do this. Breakdowns do, of course, occur, but they are exceptional.

Part of Miss Parker's evidence went as follows:

Prosecuting Counsel: Tell the jury whom you saw.
The Witness: I saw Ellen Wimslow and a man.
Prosecuting Counsel: In which direction were they walking?
The Witness: The same as I was.
Prosecuting Counsel: Could you hear them talking?

The Witness: They were talking but, apart from one word, I either could not catch or do not remember what they said.

Prosecuting Counsel: What was the word?

The Witness: Controversy. (She pronounced the word with an accent on the first and third syllables.)

Prosecuting Counsel: Who said it?

The Witness: The man.

Prosecuting Counsel: Why do you remember the word?

The Witness: Because I've always thought the correct pronunciation was *contro*versy, but recently I've heard quite a number of educated people say controversy. I'd begun to wonder if I was wrong and I noticed him use the word controversy.

Prosecuting Counsel: My Lord, I am coming back, of course, to this part of the story, but I think it will be more helpful to the jury if for the moment I invite the witness to take her mind now to the identification parade.

The Judge: Very well.

Prosecuting Counsel: Now, Miss Parker, do you remember attending an identification parade at Medlicott police station?

The Witness: Yes.

Prosecuting Counsel: Did you see a number of men?

The Witness: Yes.

Prosecuting Counsel: Did you pick out one?

The Witness: Yes.

Prosecuting Counsel: Who was it?

The Witness (pointing towards the dock): The man over there.

The Judge: You mean the prisoner?

The Witness: Yes, my Lord.

Prosecuting Counsel: Did you say anything in the prisoner's presence?

The Witness: Yes.

Prosecuting Counsel: What did you say?

The Witness: I asked him to say the word which I had written down on a piece of paper.

Prosecuting Counsel: What was the word?

The Witness: Controversy.

Prosecuting Counsel: Did the prisoner look at the piece of paper and say the word?

The Witness: Yes.

Prosecuting Counsel: How did he pronounce it?

The Witness: Controversy.

Prosecuting Counsel: Now, Miss Parker, I want to go back to what you were telling us. How far were you behind Miss Wimslow and the man when you heard the word controversy used?

The Witness: A few yards may be.

Prosecuting Counsel: I assume you could not then see their faces?

The Witness: No.

Prosecuting Counsel: Did you know then that it was Miss Wimslow?

The Witness: Yes, I know her walk and felt sure it was her.

9

Prosecuting Counsel: Go on, Miss Parker, tell us in your own words what happened.

The Witness: I was walking faster than they were and soon caught them up. I turned round as I passed them and just said " Hullo, Nell," or something like that.

Prosecuting Counsel: Could you see her face ?

The Witness: Yes.

Prosecuting Counsel: How ? It was quite dark.

The Witness: There was a street lamp about thirty yards ahead.

Prosecuting Counsel: Could you see the face of the man ?

The Witness: Fairly well.

The Judge: What do you mean by that ? You recognized your friend Miss Wimslow.

The Witness: That's really what I mean, my Lord. The light was quite sufficient to recognize anyone I knew. If I'd known the man before, I'm sure I should have recognized him.

Prosecuting Counsel: But you hadn't known him before ?

The Witness: No.

Prosecuting Counsel: Or, as far as you know, seen him ?

The Witness: No.

Prosecuting Counsel: Have you seen him since ?

The Witness: I'm sure I have.

Prosecuting Counsel: How many times ?

The Witness: Twice—that is, not counting today.

The Judge: Do you mean that since that night you have seen the man whom you saw walking that night with Miss Wimslow twice ?

The Witness: Yes.

The Judge: When ?

The Witness: Once in the police station yard at Medlicott, my Lord, and once in Court before the Magistrates.

The Judge: You mean the prisoner ?

The Witness: Yes, my Lord.

Prosecuting Counsel: Have you any doubt about it ?

The Witness: No real doubt, my Lord, but, of course, I only saw him for a moment.

Prosecuting Counsel: Did Miss Wimslow say anything to you ?

The Witness: She said much the same as I did—" Hullo, Norah " or something like that.

Prosecuting Counsel: What happened then ?

The Witness: I just walked on home.

Prosecuting Counsel: Thank you, Miss Parker, that is all I wish to ask.

Counsel for the defence then rose to cross-examine.

Defending Counsel: Miss Parker, early in your evidence you told my learned friend that you had seen a photograph of the prisoner which we know was taken ten years ago.

The Witness: Yes.

Defending Counsel: Do you think that helped you to pick out the prisoner at the identification parade?

The Witness: How do you mean "helped me"?

Defending Counsel: Do you think you could have identified him if you hadn't seen the photograph first?

The Witness: I think so, yes.

Defending Counsel: But you can't be sure?

The Witness: One can be sure of so few things.

Defending Counsel: Then you are not sure?

The Witness: I'm as sure as one can be of such things.

Defending Counsel: If you were sufficiently sure when you saw the prisoner at the parade, why did you ask him to say the word "controversy"?

The Witness: I'd mentioned the word to the inspector and he thought—

Defending Counsel: I don't want to know what the inspector thought.

The Witness: Then—?

Defending Counsel: Either you were quite sure of the prisoner's identity when you saw him or you were not? Which was it?

The Witness (after a pause): I felt as sure as I could be in my own mind.

Defending Counsel: Well—you couldn't feel sure in anyone else's mind. If you felt as sure as you did, was there any point in asking him to say the word?

The Witness: I think so, yes—a little.

Defending Counsel: Why?

The Witness: It was a help.

Defending Counsel: But you didn't need any help, did you? Or *did* you?

The Witness: I don't quite know what you mean.

Defending Counsel: Well—first of all—were you given any help to identify the prisoner?

The Witness: Given? By whom?

Defending Counsel: By anyone?

The Witness: No, certainly not.

Defending Counsel: You are quite sure of that?

The Witness: Yes—quite.

Defending Counsel: Well—if you're so sure, why did you say "by whom" when I first asked you?

The Witness: I don't know. I expect I got a bit muddled. I'm not used to giving evidence and I find it rather confusing.

Defending Counsel: I quite understand, Miss Parker, I realize it's very difficult for you. You're not used to going to police stations either, I suppose?

The Witness: Well—I have been.

Defending Counsel: Oh?

The Witness: There was a dog licence once and another time I'd left my car too long in the High Street.

Defending Counsel: I see. Have you been to Scotland Yard before as well?

The Witness: Oh no.

Defending Counsel: You found that rather frightening too, I suppose ?

The Witness: Well, they were very nice.

Defending Counsel: And they showed you a lot of photographs ?

The Witness: Yes, they did.

Defending Counsel: How quickly did you look through them ?

The Witness: I don't know exactly. I looked at them.

Defending Counsel: How many did you see altogether ?

The Witness: I don't know, but a great many.

The Judge: Give the jury some idea. Was it tens, hundreds, or thousands ?

The Witness: I should say some hundreds, my Lord.

Defending Counsel: Didn't you find that rather confusing—seeing so many different faces ?

The Witness: I don't know that it was confusing.

Defending Counsel: Your object was to identify a man whose face you had seen for perhaps one second ?

The Witness: A moment or two.

Defending Counsel: And hundreds of different faces were put in front of you ?

The Witness: Yes.

Defending Counsel: Casting your mind back, do you think some of them—apart from the one you picked out—were like the prisoner ?

The Witness: How do you mean—like the prisoner ?

Defending Counsel: Had some of them the same characteristics as the prisoner—dark hair, clean-shaven, and so on ?

The Witness: Oh—yes—some of them seemed to have dark hair and were clean-shaven.

Defending Counsel: And had ears like the prisoner ?

The Witness: I didn't particularly notice the ears.

The Judge: As far as I can see, there is nothing unusual about the prisoner's ears.

Defending Counsel: I agree, my Lord, that was my point. Many of the faces in the photographs had points in common with the prisoner's face ?

The Judge: No doubt they each had a nose, mouth, eyes, and ears, if that's what you mean, Mr. Duffield.

Defending Counsel: It is not what I mean, my Lord. Miss Parker, did not many, or at any rate some, of those photographs have faces on them which had, say, ears like those of the prisoner, eyebrows like those of the prisoner, mouths like those of the prisoner ?

The Witness: They may have.

Defending Counsel: The photograph you picked out was, as you know, taken ten years ago.

The Witness: Yes.

Defending Counsel: What was there about it which made you think it was the man you saw on the night of the murder ?

The Witness: I don't know. I just had a feeling about it.

Defending Counsel: Would you say the ears were the same ?

12

The Witness: May I see the photograph?

Defending Counsel: Not at the moment, please. I want to know what your recollection about it is first. Was it the nose, the mouth, or something else which you thought you recognized?

The Witness: I can't say without the photograph. And even with it, I may not be able to tell you anything in particular. I just felt he was the man.

Defending Counsel: You might be wrong?

The Witness: I might be, but I don't think I am.

Defending Counsel: Now perhaps you'll look at the photograph.

The Witness (after being handed the photograph): Yes?

Defending Counsel: Can you now say that there is any feature which particularly impressed you?

The Witness: No, I can't say that there was.

Defending Counsel: Now, would you be good enough to look at the prisoner—not just for a moment—but have a good look at him, please.

The Witness (after a pause while she looks at the prisoner): Yes?

Defending Counsel: Any particular feature in him which you recognized?

The Witness: I can't say there is.

Defending Counsel: It was just a moment's glance when you saw him on the common?

The Witness: A moment or so.

Defending Counsel: You had no particular reason for looking at him?

The Witness: No, but I expect I wanted to see if I knew him.

Defending Counsel: At what stage at the identification parade did you feel as sure as you could be that the prisoner was the man? After or before he said "controversy"?

The Witness: After, I suppose.

The Judge: Why do you suppose after? You must have picked him out before you asked him to say the word.

The Witness: Yes, my Lord.

The Judge: When you picked him out, how did you feel about it? Quite sure, fairly sure, uncertain, or what?

The Witness: It's difficult to analyse my feelings at the time, my Lord, but I think I must have felt fairly sure or I shouldn't have picked him out.

Defending Counsel: And then, when he said "controversy", you felt more sure?

The Witness: Yes—I suppose so.

Defending Counsel: But not absolutely sure—not as sure as you know you're giving evidence now?

The Witness: No—not as sure as that.

Defending Counsel: And before he said "controversy", you felt even less sure?

The Witness: I really don't know.

Defending Counsel: But surely it follows. If you felt more sure after-wards, you felt less sure before?

The Witness: I agree that sounds right, but it's very difficult answering questions about it now.

Defending Counsel: More or less difficult than identifying a man you'd seen for a moment?

The Witness (after a pause): I really don't know what to say to that.

Defending Counsel: I quite understand, Miss Parker—you needn't bother to answer.

Defending counsel sat down and prosecuting counsel rose to re-examine.

Prosecuting Counsel: Only just a few questions, Miss Parker. Within a week or so of your friend being killed, you went to Scotland Yard and picked out a photograph?

The Witness: Yes.

Prosecuting Counsel: Whose was it?

The Witness: The prisoner's.

Prosecuting Counsel: Did anyone give you the slightest prompting or assistance to pick it out?

The Witness: No.

Prosecuting Counsel: Within a few days of that, you went to an identi-fication parade?

The Witness: Yes.

Prosecuting Counsel: Who did you pick out there?

The Witness: The prisoner.

Prosecuting Counsel: Did anyone give you the slightest prompting or assistance to pick him out?

The Witness: No.

Prosecuting Counsel: Thank you, Miss Parker.

Then the other witnesses were called—the girl's father, the ticket collector, the waitress at the café, a pathologist, and Inspector Brooke. They gave evidence substantially in ac-cordance with counsel's opening statement. The case for the prosecution closed, and the prisoner went into the witness box.

After a few formal preliminary questions, his examination went as follows:

Defending Counsel: Mr. Essex, did you serve throughout the 1939-45 war?

The Prisoner: Yes.

Defending Counsel: I think you were twice wounded?

The Prisoner: Yes.

Defending Counsel: And twice mentioned in dispatches?

The Judge: What has this to do with the case, Mr. Duffield?
Defending Counsel: Character, my Lord.
The Judge: Well, Mr. Duffield, the responsibility is yours. I assume you appreciate what you are doing.
Defending Counsel: Absolutely, my Lord.
The Judge: Mr. Duffield, you'll forgive me if I make quite certain that you are fully aware of what I have in front of me.
Defending Counsel: I'm most grateful to your Lordship, but I am fully aware of the position.
The Judge: Very well. You may ask the question.
Defending Counsel: Thank you, my Lord.

The prisoner stated that he had been mentioned in dispatches twice and gave a short history of his life. He had been educated at Blanston College, going on from there to Cambridge. He was now in business, unmarried, lived by himself, was aged thirty-eight. With the exception of one matter, he had an exemplary character. It was that exception to which the judge was referring. He had done so in terms which the jury were not intended to understand. In most criminal cases a man's previous bad character cannot be given in evidence against him unless he attacks the character of other witnesses or gives evidence of his own good character. The judge was warning the defending counsel that if the prisoner gave evidence of his own good character, a previous conviction could be brought out in evidence. Defending counsel had decided to accept this position and to introduce the conviction himself.

Defending Counsel: You said that apart from one conviction you had always borne an exemplary character. What was the conviction for?
The Prisoner: Common assault. I was fined £10.
Defending Counsel: If necessary, are you prepared to tell my Lord and the jury the full circumstances of that case?
The Prisoner: Certainly. I lost my temper and had to pay £10 for it.
Defending Counsel: Very well. Now to deal with the facts of this case. Did you know the dead girl?
The Prisoner: No, I had never heard of her or, to the best of my knowledge, seen her.
Defending Counsel: Did you murder her?
The Prisoner: Certainly not.
Defending Counsel: Were you with her on the fifth of December last?
The Prisoner: Neither then nor on any other occasion.
Defending Counsel: Were you in Greenly on the fifth of December last?
The Prisoner: I was not.
Defending Counsel: Where were you?

The Prisoner: As I told the police, I was in Medlicott all day.

Defending Counsel: Where were you between 6 and 10 p.m. that evening?

The Prisoner: At home.

Defending Counsel: How do you live—in a house, flat, or rooms?

The Prisoner: I have a small house.

Defending Counsel: Do you live alone?

The Prisoner: Yes.

Defending Counsel: Does anyone look after you at all?

The Prisoner: I have some help every day except Saturdays and Sundays.

Defending Counsel: We know that the fifth of December was a Saturday. Do you remember what you did that day?

The Prisoner: Nothing, for the most part. I read a bit, wrote a bit, slept a bit, cooked my meals, and eventually went to bed. I was alone the whole day, as a matter of fact.

Defending Counsel: No callers?

The Prisoner: Not so far as I remember.

Defending Counsel: Thank you, Mr. Essex.

Prosecuting Counsel: So that no one can corroborate your story that you were at home at the time of the murder?

The Prisoner: It isn't my story, as you call it. It's the truth and I hope it speaks for itself.

Prosecuting Counsel: It's an unfortunate coincidence that Miss Parker thinks you were in Greenly.

The Prisoner: It is, but it isn't the first and it won't be the last.

Prosecuting Counsel: And that the ticket collector saw someone of your build go through the barrier?

The Prisoner: I don't think that's in the least unfortunate. He must have seen heaps of people of my build go through the barrier.

Prosecuting Counsel: And that you had scratched your face?

The Prisoner: Who hasn't at some time or another?

Prosecuting Counsel: At about the same time as a girl is murdered defending herself?

The Prisoner: I'm pretty certain if you asked the whole population you'd find other people had done the same thing at the same time.

Prosecuting Counsel: There's no doubt is there that the man who killed this girl assaulted her first?

The Prisoner: From what I have heard in this case and seen in the papers, there is no doubt, but I know nothing about it of my own knowledge.

Prosecuting Counsel: You do know something about assault, of your own knowledge.

The Prisoner: I've already said I once assaulted someone in a temper.

Prosecuting Counsel: A girl?

The Prisoner: A woman.

Prosecuting Counsel: A young woman?

The Prisoner: I didn't ask her age.

16

The Judge: Don't try to be funny. Did she look young or old or middle-aged?

The Prisoner: Between thirty and forty, I should say, but I don't really remember. It's some time ago.

Prosecuting Counsel: Have you assaulted so many people that you can't remember the age of this particular woman?

The Prisoner: That is the only woman I've ever assaulted and I've never assaulted a man—except, of course, in the Army—and the men I assaulted were on the other side. D'you want to know their ages?

The Judge: Don't be impertinent. You must behave yourself.

The Prisoner: I don't like counsel's hectoring manner.

The Judge: If I think you are treated unfairly, I shall intervene. So far, it is only you yourself who have behaved improperly.

The Prisoner: I'm sorry, my Lord, but I'm rather on edge. Although I'm innocent, it's a nasty position to be in.

The Judge: That I understand, but you won't help your case by being rude or pert.

Prosecuting Counsel: I ask you again—do you really mean to say that you don't know the approximate age of the only person you have ever assaulted?

The Prisoner: I've told you. Thirty to forty.

Prosecuting Counsel: I suggest to you that she was nearer twenty. Twenty-three to be exact.

The Prisoner: Well—she looked more. That's all I can say.

Prosecuting Counsel: Why did you assault her?

The Prisoner: Because I thought she had deliberately tried to trip me up. She was wheeling her bicycle on the path.

The Judge: Was it dark?

The Prisoner: Yes—my Lord. I just said to her: "You seem to want a lot of room," and the next I knew I was sent sprawling. I thought she'd tripped me up deliberately. I was very angry and when I got up I smacked her face.

Prosecuting Counsel: That wasn't her story, was it?

The Prisoner: It certainly wasn't.

Prosecuting Counsel: Didn't she suggest that you'd caught hold of her and tried to drag her off the path?

Defending Counsel: Really, my Lord, I must object. This is quite outrageous. May I consult my client so as to decide whether to apply to your Lordship for the jury to be discharged and a fresh trial begun?

The Judge: If you wish, Mr. Duffield, you may.

Prosecuting Counsel: My Lord, in my submission the evidence is admissible. Unless your Lordship rules to the contrary, I propose to ask some more questions about this. Perhaps your Lordship would think fit to ask the jury to withdraw while the matter is argued.

The Judge: Very well, Mr. Fothergill, if you want to address me on the point.

17

The jury then withdrew, and a short legal argument took place. In the case where he had been convicted, the prisoner had been charged both with assault with intent to commit a felony and with common assault. The case for the prosecution had been that the girl was walking alone with her bicycle late at night, as it had no lights. She said that the prisoner whom she did not know, came up to her and suggested going for a walk with him. She had refused, and he had then tried to drag her away. Before he had succeeded, a car came along and stopped. The girl complained to the driver, who took them both to the police. There was little corroboration of either story, but the prisoner was eventually committed for trial on both charges. The prisoner pleaded guilty to common assault and the judge who presided at his trial advised the jury that, on the evidence, it was unsafe to convict on the more serious charge. He was accordingly acquitted. Counsel for the prosecution very much wanted the jury to know of the allegation which had been made against him (it would have made another unfortunate coincidence), and he argued that, provided the whole of the circumstances of the trial were fairly put before the jury, it went to the character of the accused, and, he added, "Surely, my Lord, he can be asked whether, before assaulting the girl, he asked her to go for a walk with him." "The real object of such a question," said the judge, "must be to suggest to the jury that he was in fact guilty of the offence of which he was acquitted." After further argument, the judge refused to allow the question to be put and said that all the prisoner could be asked by the prosecution was whether he had not been fined £10 for common assault and that, while the prisoner was entitled to give his account of that assault, no evidence could be elicited by the prosecution to the contrary. After this decision, counsel for the defence decided not to ask for the jury to be discharged. The judge told them that they must altogether disregard the last question which prosecuting counsel had put about the previous trial.

After some further cross-examination, the prisoner returned to the dock and counsel addressed the jury. Counsel for the prosecution said much the same as he had said in opening the case. Counsel for the defence said this, among other things :

"My learned friend, with his usual fairness, has referred on numerous occasions and in strong language to the horrible nature of this crime, at the same time inviting you not to be thereby prejudiced. Members of the jury, I am sure that you do not feel that it is your duty to convict someone of this crime just because it has been committed. It is terrible to think that this girl's murderer is at large, but he will still be at large even if you wrongly convict my client. There have indeed been a number of these dreadful cases recently and the offender has not been brought to book. That is no reason for adding injustice to injustice and convicting someone who is entirely innocent. Supposing there had been no other such murders— would you not consider this the flimsiest murder case you have ever heard of? And, if so, is it any stronger because there have been other murders? What is the real evidence against my client? The belief by Miss Parker that she saw my client with the dead girl? Is that the kind of evidence upon which to convict a man of any criminal offence—murder or any other?"

Duffield went on for some time, strongly emphasizing the absence of proof, and eventually sat down. Then the judge summed up. He told the jury what were the ingredients of the crime of murder, that they must feel sure of his guilt before they convicted the prisoner, that it was for the prosecution to make them feel sure and not for the defence to make them feel uncertain, and he went into the evidence in detail. Finally, he asked them to consider their verdict.

"Before we retire," said the foreman, who was a professor of metaphysics, "may I ask your Lordship for some enlightenment?"

"What is your question?" asked the judge.

"Your Lordship said that before the jury can convict we must feel sure of the prisoner's guilt. May I ask your Lordship exactly what 'feel sure' means?"

"It means what it says," said the judge, rather testily. "Before you can convict, you must feel quite sure."

"I'm sorry to trouble your Lordship," went on the foreman, "but I still would be grateful for some help. The jury feel quite sure they are trying this case. Have they to be as sure of the prisoner's guilt as that?"

"No, of course not," said the judge.

"Well, my Lord, when I asked your Lordship what 'sure' meant, you said 'quite sure', but now you seem to be saying that it means 'not quite sure'. It's a little confusing for the jury. I always used to read that the prosecution had to prove its case beyond all reasonable doubt."

"So it has," said the judge, and he added, recognizing a look on the foreman's face, "you may not ask me what that means." The judge paused, thought for a moment, and then said: "Members of the jury, on consideration I think your foreman's original question was a very sensible one. I can best answer it by saying that, before convicting a man, a jury must feel as sure of his guilt as they can feel sure of anything which they have not plainly seen for themselves."

The jury retired, the prisoner was taken to the cells, and counsel went to the robing room.

"It's really a scandal," said Fothergill. "He'll get away with it again."

"I don't know," said Duffield. "There have been so many of these murders, the jury might take the bit between their teeth."

"Not on this evidence. Unless I could break him down or get in that original charge, I knew I was done. But there it is. I've done my best to save the life of the next girl he takes for a walk."

"And I suppose you'll say I've done my best to kill her."

"Well, you have really, but that's the way things are. Someone's got to defend the man, and no doubt he's assured you of his innocence."

"I must say he's been pretty casual about it. That's one of the things in his favour. There's been none of those 'you do believe me, don't you' remarks or constant assertions of innocence which you usually find with guilty people. He just told me he'd had nothing to do with it and says that naturally he expects to get off."

"Well—he will, but he's guilty all right. Don't you think so?"

"Yes, I do really, but I can't exactly say why."

In the jury room the acquittal of the prisoner was very far from being a foregone conclusion.

"I suggest," said the foreman, "that before we discuss the matter, we take a provisional vote—secret to begin with. If you agree, will you all write down Guilty, Not Guilty, or Undecided, and screw up the piece of paper and put it in this hat?"

The remainder of the jury agreed to the suggestion, with the result that their provisional vote disclosed three for Guilty, one for Not Guilty, and eight Undecided.

"Humph," said the foreman, after he'd announced the result. "Pity this room isn't more comfortable. We may be here some time."

"I can't think why," said one man. "That girl was obviously telling the truth."

"Of course she was," said another, "but that doesn't mean she was right. She only saw him for a moment."

"She picked out his picture."

"And if she was wrong about that, we hang an innocent man. Once she'd picked out the picture, she was pretty well bound to identify him in the police station."

"What about controversy? I'm blessed if I know how to pronounce it, but it's an odd coincidence."

"Is it? Ask anyone here how they pronounce it. You'll find a bias in favour of controversy."

They tried it and they did.

"Pretty dreadful to hang a man just because he pronounces a word wrong."

"Or right perhaps."

"If we let him go, he may kill someone else."

"The judge says we mustn't consider that. The only question is whether his guilt is proved in this case."

Two hours later the jury were still undecided.

CHAPTER II

THE EXECUTION

THE cocktail party given by Laura Duffield was in full swing when her husband returned home. There was an immediate silence as he came into the room. Everyone wanted to know the result of the trial.

"Well?" said Laura.

"He got away," said her husband.

"You devil," said Laura.

"It wasn't me," said her husband modestly. "There wasn't enough evidence."

"Let's hope there is next time," volunteered a guest.

"What a horrible thing to say. That means there'll be a next time."

"There probably will be. He obviously did it, and the others. I don't know why the jury weren't allowed to be told about them."

"Well," said Duffield, "they knew about them all right. That was one of my troubles, but it was a good jury, they really did put them out of their minds. But it took them two and a half hours to do it, or I'd have been home earlier. Let's have a drink. I'm dying for one."

"I think it's a disgrace," said a girl. "No woman under forty will be safe going home alone."

"I'll take you," said the man next to her.

"Will that be safe?"

"Well—safer. I don't kill my victims."

"I've an idea," said a young man. "Why not manufacture luminous signs to be worn by girls at night with 'I'm over forty' on them? You could do some good advertising. How about: 'Lucy was always being attacked until she wore one of these'?"

"I don't think it's in the least funny," said Alison Hepworth, a tall fair-haired girl of twenty. "At least four are dead already. At least two of them were decent girls from decent homes. I think it's dreadful and something should be done about it. It's certainly nothing to laugh about."

"I'm sorry, Alison," said the young man, suddenly abashed. "You're quite right. D'you think dreadfully of me for what I said? It just slipped out."

"No—not dreadfully— just that you must be very young."

This was true. Robert Archer was nineteen, and he had adored Alison for quite three months. And now she had told him he was very young. She could not have said anything to hurt him more. Still, he was old enough to die for his country. He would gladly do so and then perhaps she'd be sorry. But there wasn't a war on. Or he'd die for her. But, again, there was no immediate opportunity. Meanwhile he must do something about it.

"Yes," he said, "I'm afraid I am. I'm terribly sorry. I wish I could do something about it. When I was a small boy I always wanted to be seventeen. I always looked upon seventeen as grown-up. Now I want to be twenty-one. I wonder what I'll want to be when I'm twenty-one. And I wonder how old one has to be before one starts wanting to knock off the years instead of adding them on."

Alison smiled.

"You're quite sweet, Bobbie, really," she said.

From being in the depths of despair he was now immediately at the top of the ladder.

"D'you mean that?" he said seriously.

"Don't be so tense, Bobbie," she said, "or I'll be frightened to say anything to you."

He was down a rung or two.

In another corner of the room a man of thirty-five was talking to Duffield.

"Don't you feel a bit awkward when you think your client is guilty? I know that it's right that you should defend him, whatever you think yourself, or he wouldn't be defended at all, but I should have thought it was pretty hard on you."

"Oh, I don't know, Alec, one gets used to it. As a matter of fact, in most cases one feels it's a feather in one's cap to get a man off in cases like that. It's when I think my client may be innocent that I get really worried in case I don't get him off. But that doesn't often happen. If they're innocent, they don't often get as far as me."

"What sort of a chap is Essex?"

"Too smooth for my liking. Not a fool by any means, and nothing about him which pronounced him a murderer. I didn't much care for his mouth. But it's awfully easy when you know a man's accused of a crime to read things into his face. In fact it's a very dangerous thing to try to judge a man by his face. I've been caught several times myself. I've had civil cases where I've known there was a villain on the other side. When I've gone into Court I've looked round the Court to find him. Until I learned not to do so, I used to find someone who clearly looked the most unprincipled ruffian. Usually he turned out to be a most respectable solicitor. After a few mistakes like that, I gave it up. Your glass is empty."

"I've been doing well before you came. Must have had at least half a dozen—and they're strong."

"Well—you haven't got to work afterwards. Laura—Alec's dying for a drink—when you've finished over there."

Alec Morland looked round the room. He felt like an adventure. He was an artist of independent means and a bachelor. He was not a successful artist, but he enjoyed painting and occasionally sold a picture. On the other hand, he was a most successful bachelor and, although he had had some narrow escapes, he had so far managed to retain his status. Marriage was one thing, adventure another. During the war he had had many and varied adventures of a different kind. He started in the infantry; then he joined a special service battalion; then he became a Commando. He was strong physically and one of the comparatively few people who enjoyed danger. He had killed men silently and quickly with his own hands, and he had been decorated for doing so. It makes such a difference how and when you kill. If you kill the right person at the right time, you are publicly acclaimed as a hero. But mistake the person or the time and you will very likely be hanged. But it was not this type of adventure which he wanted at that moment, although, as he glanced round the room, he did not at first notice an obvious opportunity for any other. But, as Laura filled his glass, he saw enough to ask for an introduction.

"That's Jill Whitby. She's sweet," said Laura. "Come along."

While the cocktail party was proceeding in the normal way, Gilbert Essex was going home. Medlicott and Cunningham are about forty miles apart. When he reached Medlicott, he called in at several public houses on the way to his house, but he did not become in the least drunk. He was extremely pleased with himself. Of course he had been anxious during the jury's retirement, and, indeed, on many occasions since his arrest, but throughout he had felt that it would be all right in the end. His counsel seemed quietly confident, and, as he listened to the evidence, his own confidence increased. And now he was safe. How good it was to be free and to feel sure of the future. But he must be more careful. He had never thought that the girl who said "Hullo" would have been able to recognize him. He wouldn't make the same mistake again. If he were seen by anyone with his intended victim near the place where she was to die, in future he would let her go. After all, it was easy enough provided you were careful to choose different districts. What a pity, he thought, that I shall never be able to see my reminiscences in print. He had started these some years previously and they were kept in a place in his house where it was humanly impossible that the police would ever look. Unless they had some reason to tear the house apart, brick by brick and board by board. And they never had had and never would have such a reason. He never took his victims near his home, let alone inside it. He usually left them in the place he had killed them, though sometimes, if it was near enough, he would throw the lady in a river, down a pit, or in a ditch. But this was not essential.

He passed a policeman.

"Good night, officer," he said.

"Good night, sir."

He passed a girl. It was much too near home, but it did occur to him that it would make excellent reading next morning if he could kill someone on the way home after his acquittal.

But it wouldn't do. Too dangerous. He wasn't going to Cunningham Assizes again. Nor any other—the Old Bailey or anywhere else. A little more care in future. Twice he'd slipped up. The assault case and this one. It was a pity they had his photograph at Scotland Yard. And now they'd have a recent one—though not the official front face and side face. But good enough to be recognized. Yes—he'd learned his lesson—and at comparatively small expense. Duffield's fees and the solicitor's costs were not all that high. But it must not occur again. He longed to write his story for the Press and it was exasperating that he could not do so. But his work would be published—after his death, and he had to console himself with imagining the sensation it would cause. A problem he would have to face was how to ensure its publication without making it available as evidence against him during his lifetime. Still, there was plenty of time to solve that. Probably the best solution would be to put it in a safe deposit. What part, he wondered, would the public read most eagerly? He decided to add a paragraph or two when he got home. And later that evening he wrote:

"I think perhaps I get the greatest pleasure when I take out some completely innocent girl who sees no harm in going for a stroll with a chance acquaintance in broad daylight. Suddenly I say to her: 'How d'you know I'm not a murderer?' and make a movement towards her as though to strangle her. Her sudden fear and equally sudden relief, when I move back with a smile, I find quite delightful. I repeat this two or three times. Sometimes it makes them anxious, sometimes confident. Finally, I say to them quite quietly: 'As a matter of fact—I am going to kill you', and this time I don't draw back. I consider a murder of this kind a work of art. These are my Monets or Renoirs or Van Goghs. They are not always possible. One cannot always have perfection. But when they are perfect, there is a rhythm about them which I find irresistible. Distortion there must be sometimes. A mild form I call a Modigliani. But sometimes things go wrong and there is complete distortion. They are still representational—nothing abstract about them at all, but the rhythm is lacking, or perhaps it would be more correct to say that instead of the gently flowing stream which ends in the glorious cascade, it is a rhythm of jerks, like machinery gone wrong. But it always ends the same way. She is dead."

He slept well and peacefully that night.

Three weeks later he killed again. The murder was of exactly the same kind as that for which he had been tried. But this time he had been more careful. There was not a scrap of evidence against him.

"The police have interviewed a man whom they think may be able to help them in their inquiries," said the newspapers discreetly. This referred to the fact that the police had called on Gilbert Essex to see if they could by legitimate methods persuade him to give himself away. He answered their questions politely and, from their point of view, most unsatisfactorily, and at the end he said:

"I do think it rotten bad luck, Inspector, that just because I've been acquitted of one murder you should always suspect me when there's another. But, human nature being what it is, I suppose I can't blame you. Anything more you'd like to know, Inspector?"

"We don't *always* suspect you," said the inspector. "And anyway there's only been one murder of the same kind since you were acquitted."

"So there has, Inspector. Only one. Well, let's hope there aren't any more."

And he left it for two months before making it two.

Again there was no evidence. The public became anxious. Questions were asked in the House. The police themselves felt embarrassed.

"Why don't you catch Mr. Essex instead of bothering about me?" asked a motorist when charged by a constable with obstruction.

And then one day, when public anxiety was at its height, it was suddenly relieved. The B.B.C. actually interrupted a sports commentary by making this announcement:

"Gilbert Essex, who was acquitted of murder some months ago, has been found dead."

CHAPTER III

THE EXECUTIONER

IT was plainly a case of murder. He had been struck on the head, his unconscious body dragged to the edge of a cliff and thrown over. The fall had killed him. The police now had to make inquiries of a different kind, but they could not help feeling grateful to the man for whom they were looking. But, whatever crimes the victim may have committed—treason, murder, or blackmail, or all three—no private person can be allowed to take the law into his own hands and kill him. He must be killed by the hangman or by no one.

Alec Morland was sitting in his house in Cunningham talking to Jill Whitby about a matter of considerable importance to them both when the bell rang and Chief-Inspector Curtis of the Cunningham police asked for an interview.

"Would you like me to go?" asked Jill.

"Oh—I don't think that will be necessary," said the inspector. "I thought Mr. Morland might be able to help me in some inquiries I'm making."

"What can I do for you, Inspector?" said Alec.

"It's about this Essex case. I suppose people don't realize that we have to investigate his murder just as thoroughly as the murders he committed?"

"Murders?"

"Yes, sir, murders. You'll get a shock when you read the papers in a day or two. I can't say any more at the moment. In the meantime, we've got to find the hero who got rid of him. Personally I'd give him a George Medal."

"Have you any idea who it is?"

"Not the slightest, sir, at the moment. What we're doing at present is to eliminate. It's a cumbersome process, but, in default of direct information, it's the only course open to us. We know when Essex was killed and I have here a list of people who were seen the night he was killed in a place where theoretically they might have been if they'd killed him. I hope I'm making myself plain, sir, and I'd like to assure you, sir, that in your case the inquiry is only a formality. P.C. Carthew says he saw you that night in Adam Lane. Would that be correct, sir?"

"Yes, I think so," said Alec, after hesitating for a moment. "Yes, I remember I did see him. He was on a bicycle."

"That's right, sir. Now, would you mind just telling me where you'd come from when he saw you? I do apologize for troubling you, but it'll enable me to eliminate one of the names we've got."

"Am I a suspect then?"

"Good gracious, no, sir. But, if we leave anyone out, the system's no use. It isn't much use anyway in a case like this, but we haven't anything else to go on."

"Nothing at all?"

"Nothing really. We found a bit of pencil at the place where the body was thrown over, but that doesn't look like being very helpful. You don't use Royal Sovereign pencils by any chance, do you, sir?"

"Well, I expect I do sometimes, Inspector, and I bite the ends."

"D'you mean that, sir?" inquired the inspector, and then added: "But I suppose a lot of people do."

"You mean the bit you've found was a bitten Royal Sovereign?"

"Well, it is, as a matter of fact."

"Well, Inspector," said Alec, "I'd better tell you at once that I do carry a pencil in my waistcoat pocket, and I suppose it might have slipped out when I threw the body over."

"You didn't, I suppose, sir?"

"No, Inspector, I didn't, but it just shows how careful one must be not to leave things lying about in case someone commits a murder there."

The inspector smiled.

"I'm sorry, sir," he said, "but we can't afford to overlook

anything. Even your statement about the pencil I'll have to report."

"Dear, dear," said Alec, "I shall get quite nervous. Now, what else was there you wanted to ask me?"

"Just where you'd come from, sir, when you met P.C. Carthew."

"Oh yes, of course. I hadn't come from anywhere really. I'd just been for a stroll."

"Starting from?"

"Here."

"And going to?"

"Down Adam Lane and back again. I often go there."

"Did you get as far as the cliff?"

"I don't think so. Let me think. No, I didn't that night."

"How long were you out altogether, sir?"

"Half an hour or so. I can't be precise about that."

"No, of course not."

"Did you happen to see a young lady at any time that evening?"

"Several I expect—in the town."

"In Adam Lane?"

"Not that I recall. It's conceivable. I was thinking about something, as a matter of fact, so I might not have noticed."

"And, of course, you never saw the dead man?"

"Not so far as I know, Inspector, but, of course, I might not have noticed him either."

"You didn't see a man and a girl together?"

"Not so far as I know. But I wouldn't swear I didn't."

"Well—thank you very much, sir. I'm sorry I've had to take so much of your time. I'm afraid I may have to trouble you once more about the pencil. Could you perhaps come down to the station some time to see it?"

"Yes, of course, Inspector. Tomorrow do?"

"Thank you very much, sir. Any particular time?"

"About eleven?"

"That's very good of you, sir. And thank you very much indeed for your help. I'm so sorry to have bothered you."

"Not at all, Inspector. Good night."

As soon as the inspector had left, Alec said: "Now what was I saying when we had that silly interruption?"

"As far as I can remember, you were asking me to marry you—but it seems such a long time ago I might have made a mistake."

Alec paused for a moment. Then:

"Yes, it is rather a long time ago, isn't it? Still—I think I'll ask it just the same."

"I'm so glad you remembered, my darling," she said.

Then there was silence for a little time, broken only by the usual noises. During a lull she said:

"I do love you, Alec. I shall be terribly happy with you. I know it. I've waited so long for you, you know. You are my first and only love. You know that, don't you?"

"I do. And so are you mine—though I'm afraid there are a good many people who would dispute that."

"It all depends what you mean by love. You're my first in every sense."

"And you're mine in the best sense."

There was another qualified silence.

"We shall be so happy."

"Yes, we shall."

"We'll be married soon?"

"Very soon."

"How glorious."

"How long have we been engaged?"

"Hours, it seems."

"Ever since that inspector went. It wasn't your pencil, I suppose?"

There was a ring at the bell. Alec started slightly. Then he went to the door. It was only his next door neighbour wanting to borrow something.

"That inspector's made you quite jumpy, darling," said Jill, when he came back. "D'you know, you lost colour for a moment."

"Did I? How silly."

There was uninterrupted silence for a moment. Then Jill said suddenly and quite seriously: "It wasn't you, was it, darling?"

31

Alec said nothing. This time Jill went white.

"I think I'm going to faint, darling," she said.

He took her in his arms. She did not faint but stayed there, silent and terrified. He tried to comfort her and then said:

"Would you like me to go away and never come back?"

"Oh—not that, darling. That's what terrifies me so. We're so happy. I don't mind what you've done—but I can't bear to lose you."

"Shall I tell you about it?"

"Not if you'd rather not."

"It's better for you to hear, if you can. I'll give you back your word at the end, if you want it."

"I don't care what you tell me. You will always be mine, always. Oh, please don't let them take you away. We're so happy."

"Now—don't be too upset, darling. I'm sure it'll be all right. That was only a routine call. There's nothing against me really. And I want you to know."

"Go on, darling. Tell me."

"I'd thought about it in a vague sort of way ever since the Duffield cocktail party. You know I did a lot of killing in the war—sometimes single-handed. I killed decent people—people like Duffield himself perhaps—people who were of use in the world—who had something to give to it—people who weren't just there to see what they could get out of it. And in fact they gave their lives. Well—it had to be done. And I can't pretend I found it difficult. Partly one worked up a hate, and partly it was self-preservation. Kill or be killed. I'm afraid, too, I often enjoyed the excitement."

"You did marvellously, darling. I know all about you, you know, though you've never said a word about it."

"I did no better than hundreds of other people and I had luck. Well, at that Duffield party, the casual way in which one or two people talked about Essex's next victim exasperated me. I wasn't angry with Duffield. Of course not. He did his job. Someone had to. No doubt there was a lack of evidence. But it seemed so dreadful that a murderer of that kind should be let loose to kill again. I felt sure he would—and he did. Not

32

once, but twice. And I assure you that, if he had been alive now, there'd have been a third."

"D'you mean the girl the inspector mentioned?"

"I do."

"Did she see you?"

"No, I'm sure she couldn't have. I'll come to that in a minute."

"I'm sorry, darling, I shouldn't have interrupted—but I'm so terribly—terribly anxious. Oh—darling."

He kissed her for some time, and then went on:

"When the next murder after his acquittal happened, I said to myself, like many other people, 'This man ought to be put out of the way.' Easy to say. The police were trying hard enough, I'm sure—but nothing happened except another murder. The sense of frustration was appalling. I decided that something must be done about it. If the police couldn't catch him, I would. I took a room in a hotel in Medlicott where Essex lived, and I shadowed him. Nothing happened for the first few days, but, on the day he died, he took a train for Cunningham in the evening. I went too, in another carriage. He went into a public house and eventually came out with a girl. They went towards a wood not far from the cliff. I followed. It was quite dark now. I think you'll find he always chooses moonless nights. Or chose, I should say. My original intention had been to arrest him, and I had a spanner with me in case he proved too tough a proposition for me. And then I realized that, unless I let him kill or attack the girl, there was nothing I could arrest him for. The police would have been in exactly the same position. Besides, if I let him start to assault her, he could only get a prison sentence. But I couldn't even allow that; it would have been too cruel to the girl. If I intervened before he did anything, I couldn't have arrested him at all. It's no crime to walk with a girl in a wood. Even if your name is Gilbert Essex. It was a ridiculous position. There I was and there was in effect nothing I could do except save one girl's life. That, of course, I should certainly do, but he'd have gone off scot free and some other girl would have been killed later. The object of capital punishment is to save innocent lives. At any rate that's the main argument of those who believe in its

33

retention. It may deter a potential murderer from killing. So the public, through the medium of a judge, a jury, and hangman, kills people. There was only one way in which an innocent life could be saved on this occasion—I don't mean the life of the girl he was with—as I've said, it was easy to save her—but the one after her could only be saved if I struck first. Between her death and the unhappiness of her parents, family, and friends there stood me and me only—and my spanner. I made up my mind to use it. They sat down in the wood. I could hear them talking. I was behind a bush between ten and twenty yards away. And then I spoke. Not too loud, but loud enough for them to hear.

" 'The man you are with is Gilbert Essex. Get up and run.'

"They stopped talking at once.

" 'Go on,' I said, 'run for your life.'

"And she did. She couldn't, of course, have told whether it was a practical joke or not, but she was taking no chances. As soon as she'd gone, I went up to him. He was starting to get up. I hit him hard on the head. He sank to the ground. I dragged him to the edge of the wood. There was no one to be seen. Visibility was, of course, very bad, but I could hear no one about either. I dragged him a hundred yards or so to the edge of the cliff and pushed him over. It's a nice long drop and was bound to kill him. I'd done the same to a German in 1942. I must say I had the same feeling of satisfaction this time. I straightened my tie, put the spanner in my pocket and strolled home through Adam Lane. There I met a policeman on a bicycle. I came home, washed the spanner, and went to bed. The next day I went to Medlicott and fetched my things. Now, what d'you think of me?"

"I love you, darling, but not more, because that's impossible."

There was another ring at the bell.

CHAPTER IV

VISITING

AMBROSE LOW sat at home reading a financial paper without much enthusiasm. He was in the middle of a strange life. It started with his birth some thirty-six years before. There had been nothing particularly strange about that. Indeed, the strangeness only began when he was between twenty and twenty-five, when he took to a life of crime with the greatest enthusiasm. He was a man of the highest intelligence and he brought a degree of ingenuity and forethought to his profession which must have been unrivalled. At any rate, it is to be hoped so. He was never caught. At the age of thirty-five, when he might be said to have been at the height of his career, it was suddenly ended by a series of events which resulted in his procuring the acquittal of a High Court judge, Mr. Justice Prout, who was mistakenly accused of murder, and in his marrying the beautiful daughter of the judge, Elizabeth. She was an exquisite creature, with a brain to match her husband's. For a variety of reasons it became necessary for Mr. Low to live a respectable life after his marriage to Elizabeth, and, as he had no actual convictions and was married to a judge's daughter, he had no difficulty in becoming a stockbroker. Elizabeth chose this new career for him. They were comfortably off and it seemed as good as any. They were very happy together. It does not often work out that two equally strong-minded and intelligent people can live happily together, but in this case it worked very well. Husbands and wives, after years of living together, are often able to read each other's thoughts without much difficulty, but Elizabeth and her husband started life together as though they had lived together for a century. Each could spot the thoughts of the other with uncanny precision. Hardly a word had to be said. A look, a

35

movement, the slightest inflexion in the voice or the accentuation of a word which a normal person would not have noticed, was enough for either of them. Perforce they had no secrets from one another.

Mr. Low took to stockbroking as he had taken to crime. He applied his intelligence to the job and, as far as was possible, his ingenuity, but he found much less scope for this last quality. This disappointed him. He liked to invent and devise—not machines but courses of action, trains of events. Something could be done on the Stock Exchange but not enough. He was very happy with Elizabeth, but something was missing. So, when he answered the door to an attractive young woman who was a complete stranger to him and she asked for Mr. Ambrose Low, he was pleased. It was a Saturday afternoon, Elizabeth had gone to see her father and she had told him that he ought to read certain leading articles. But his visitor, who was Jill Whitby, seemed much more promising.

"I'm terribly sorry to trouble you," she began.

"Come in and sit down," he said. "I'm delighted to see a strange face. Have a cigarette." Jill sat down and waited for a moment. It was a little difficult to know how to begin. At last she started with :

"It's really gross impertinence on my part. I want to ask your advice. Are you sure you don't mind ?"

"My dear Miss——"

"Whitby."

"My dear Miss Whitby, I do not even want to know why you came or who sent you. As long as you don't want to ask about stocks and shares, my advice, such as it is, is at your disposal."

"But I must tell you. Or you won't understand. You were the private inquiry agent who took such a prominent part in the trial of Mr. Justice Prout. I read all about it."

"So did I. I thought it made very good reading, as a matter of fact. Mr. Justice Prout is now my father-in-law."

"Yes, I know."

"I like to remind myself of the fact. So I say it every now and then. But you haven't come for my autograph or anything so banal as that, I hope."

36

"Oh—no—I'm terribly worried and I thought you might be able to help."

"Now we're talking," said Mr. Low. "My entire service is at your disposal. Elizabeth won't be home just yet. I'm not sure that she'd approve. So fire ahead."

"Suppose—only suppose—mind you—someone—like Mr. Justice Prout for instance—were suspected of a murder he hadn't committed—is there anything he could do about it?"

"I'm afraid that's far too general a question. You must be much more precise. What have you done, or, rather, what haven't you done?"

"Oh—it isn't me."

"Well, that's something. But there are a lot of other people in the world besides you. Perhaps you'd better tell me who it is who didn't do what."

Jill hesitated.

"How do I know that I can trust you?" she asked.

"You don't, but, as the person concerned hasn't done whatever it is, it doesn't seem to matter much. Anyway, I can't think why you came here if you were only going to talk in riddles."

"You're quite right, but I feel awful. I'm terribly unhappy."

"Take a deep breath and out with it."

Jill hesitated.

"That's the best way, I assure you," he added.

"All right," she said. "I'm terrified my fiancé will be charged with the murder of Gilbert Essex. He didn't do it, of course."

"Of course not. Which is why you're so worried. Of course, if he'd done it, you'd have nothing more to do with him."

Jill said nothing.

"Or very little. Well—I must say—he did—I mean he didn't do a very good job of work."

"D'you think so?"

"I do indeed. So will everyone. But, of course, it can't be allowed. That's your view, no doubt. Lucky he didn't do it. Why are you so worried about him being suspected?"

"Well, an inspector called to see him."

"I see. What did he want?"

Jill told him.

"Is there any other evidence against him?"

"Not that I know of, but, of course, there may be. And what so terrifies me is the thought of living always with the possibility of his being arrested in front of me. We shall never be able to feel safe—never. We may be married for years—have children—and then one day there may be a knock at the door and—and—why only yesterday we were together and I was terrified because there was a ring at the bell. It was nothing, as it happened—but the thought of fearing every knock or ring for the rest of our lives is too dreadful. It makes me feel quite sick."

"But if nothing happens for a year or two, everything should be all right. And perhaps they'll catch the real murderer. Had you never thought of that?"

"No—I suppose I hadn't. But suppose they don't—even if years do go by, there's nothing to stop them taking proceedings if they get the evidence, is there?"

"No—there isn't, but sometimes they close cases, don't they?"

"But they can open them again, I suppose?"

"Yes—I suppose they can. I see your point."

"And it might affect the children, too. If from time to time I'm worrying about it, they may be born with all sorts of complexes. I know that very little is really known about that sort of thing, but it's a horrifying thought. They might be insane."

"Have another cigarette," said Mr. Low, "and let me think for a moment." There was a pause. "Tell me your friend's name and address," he said, after thinking for a few minutes.

Jill told him.

"Now, is there anything you haven't told me?"

Jill did not answer at once.

"I see," said Mr. Low. "Don't bother."

"What d'you mean?"

"Oh—nothing. I just don't want you to distress yourself too much by saying more than is good for you. I'm terribly sorry for you, you know. I really am."

"Thank you very much. You're very kind."

"It's natural. Anyone would be."

There was silence for a few minutes.

"All right," said Mr. Low at last. "There's only one thing to do. Go home and forget it. Innocent men don't get convicted of murder. They're seldom charged. My father-in-law was an extraordinary exception."

"But is that all you can do for us? Go home and forget it? You know I can't."

"You must try. I'm afraid there's nothing else to be done, at the moment. I really am most awfully sorry for you both—but I'm sure it'll be all right in the end."

"What d'you mean by 'at the moment'?"

"What I say. For the present go home and try to forget it. I may call on your fiancé."

"But I haven't told him I've been to you. He might not approve."

"Well—I should, if I were you. But, anyway, I won't say anything about it if I do call, unless I know he knows. Now try to cheer up. I expect it'll be all right in the end."

"In the end?" said Jill. "When will that be? When we're both dead. But, thank you very much all the same. You have been kind."

A few minutes later she left Mr. Low. She was sorry she had been to see him. He had been kind but useless, and she had probably talked too much for no purpose.

Within a moment or two of Jill leaving, Elizabeth returned. She kissed her husband.

"Poor lonely man," she said. "Who was she?"

"As a matter of fact, she's going to marry the man who killed Gilbert Essex."

"Ambrose," said Elizabeth sternly, "you leave it alone."

"How you jump to conclusions. I merely told you who the girl was."

"That's true enough. You didn't add that she came to you for help."

"I didn't get a chance. She's worried to bits, poor girl. Says it'll be hanging over them for ever."

"I don't think the word hanging is appropriate in this case. He's a public benefactor."

"I agree, my sweet, but the public can't accept benefits of that kind. And your father a judge. I'm surprised at you."

"I suppose it will be hanging over them unless he's caught. The Home Secretary would commute the sentence though."

"I dare say, but to have a commutable death sentence hanging over a newly married couple, with the certainty of some years of imprisonment if he were caught, would be most upsetting. I shouldn't like it anyway. How about you?"

"There's nothing you can do anyway."

"I'm not so sure," said Mr. Low. There was a pause, then he added: "He oughtn't to have done it, ought he? Much as I admire his public spiritedness, he oughtn't to have done it. Where's your law and order? Much more important than a few people's lives. If one were allowed to kill undesirables, no one would be safe. Why, my dear, someone might have a go at me some time—by mistake, of course."

"What are you getting at?"

"A crime's been committed—murder—and I've been told about it. Isn't it my duty to go to the police? Of course, she said he didn't do it, but we know all about that, don't we, my love? As a law-abiding citizen, don't you think I ought to go to the police? That poor girl, she looked so unhappy. Don't you think I ought to?"

Elizabeth thought for a moment or two.

"All right," she said. "You win. But it's only because I hate to see you fidgeting."

"And what better reason, my angel, could there possibly be?"

"Many, I should think. D'you find stockbroking terribly dull?"

"Oh, it's all right, but I get a bit tired of some of the types, particularly the ones that sidle up to you with a story which is probably only a vulgar version of a clean one I've already heard. 'I say, old man, I've got one for you.' It makes me shudder."

"At any rate, they're perfectly honest, decent people. They can't go to gaol for telling them."

"Some of them ought to. And, anyway, do you think it kind to rake up what you mistakenly believe to be my murky past, my sweet?"

"In some ways I preferred you when you were a crook. I resent the high moral tone from you sometimes."

"And I resent nothing—not even your marrying me or calling me names."

He kissed her.

"My sweet darling," he went on, "let me tell you something. I would cheerfully rob the Bank of England—that, at any rate, is honest and above board. Nothing underhanded about it. But some of the things that happen in the City—they horrify me. They do go to gaol sometimes, of course, or, if the thing comes off, they get knighted. That's big business."

"Since you retired from crime you seem to think that you're the only honest person in the world."

"There we go again. Retired from crime indeed! But I seem to remember that my last crimes—if they were crimes—which I dispute—were very helpful to your father, my sweet, if I may mention such a subject."

"What do you propose to do about your lovely visitor?"

"I didn't say she was lovely."

"No, my darling, but I saw her. Don't you think she's lovely?"

"Quite good looking, I should say—yes, I think it's fair to say that."

"Well, I should say it was neither fair nor true. But, never mind, I'm not jealous—yet. What are you going to do about her?"

"About her? Nothing."

"About her fiancé then?"

"I shall pay him a call, I suppose."

"A sort of return visit?"

"Something of the kind."

"And then?"

"We shall see."

"You mean *you* will."

"I mean *we*. Have I ever been able to keep anything from you?"

"Well, have you?"

They continued their verbal tennis match for some minutes. Then they adjourned for tea.

Two days later Mr. Low called on Alec. "My name is Low," he said. "Ambrose Low. I'm not a police officer, nor an inquiry agent, but a stockbroker."

"I had an idea," said Alec, "that peddling shares is no longer allowed."

"Quite right. It isn't and that's not what I'm here for."

"Then may I ask— ?" Alec paused and waited for an answer.

"Indeed you may. I've come to see you about the late Gilbert Essex."

"May I ask what his death has to do with you?"

"I had nothing to do with his death—except that I rejoiced to hear of it, like most people. You did, I suppose?"

"Did what?"

"Rejoiced."

"I suppose so."

"Good. Then we've that in common. Let's see if we've anything else. The police are looking for the man who killed him. There's no evidence against me. What about you? Have we that in common too?"

"Before we continue this conversation, I'd like to know what business it is of yours."

"I should like to help the man who did it, that's all."

"Then why come here?"

"You tell me," said Mr. Low. "You should know better than me. Don't you?"

"I've no idea who you are or what you are or why you're here. Oh—I suppose—you heard that a police inspector called here. Is that it? Oh—of course—you're from the Press. Want a story, I suppose."

"Yes—I'd like a story. But I'm not from the Press. I told you my name. I was to some extent responsible for the acquittal of Mr. Justice Prout."

"I remember, but I still fail to see what it's got to do with me."

"At this rate I shall be here some time."

"You won't, I assure you. I should like you to go now."

"I'm not surprised you're a bit on edge," said Mr. Low, "but it's awfully difficult to help you if you don't confide in me. I might make an awful mess of it."

"Of what?"

"Of everything. I hate innocent people being convicted. Or some guilty people, if it comes to that. Could you bear to tell me what evidence there is against you? I'm not asking for any admissions, you understand. I just want to know what could be proved against you if the police get busy."

"I'll make any statement there is to be made to the police," said Alec, "and I must wish you a very good afternoon."

"Oh—well," said Mr. Low, "I'm glad to have broken the ice anyway."

Later Alec told Jill of Mr. Low's visit.

"I'm afraid it looks like blackmail," he said. "I can't think of any other reason. I thought he was from the Press at first, but I'm sure he can't be."

"Did he say who he was?"

"He said he was Ambrose Low—you know—the chap who had a good deal to do with old Prout's case—but I dare say it wasn't him at all. It's very worrying—blackmail. Of course he didn't ask for anything this time, but I suppose that's their way as often as not. Came on a fishing expediiton, as far as I can see. At any rate, he caught nothing."

Jill didn't speak for a moment. Then she told Alec of her visit to Mr. Low.

"I know I ought to have told you before, darling, but I didn't know what to do for the best, and I did so want to help."

"That's all right, darling," said Alec, "but how d'you think he can help?"

"I've no idea. I just had a feeling that I must do something. This waiting and wondering if something's going to happen is so unnerving. And it'll go on like this for ever. I don't know what to do—I really don't."

"All right, my darling, if it'll make you feel happier, I'll see him again. Would you like me to?"

"I just don't know. My mind's been in such a whirl ever since you told me that I don't really know what to think or what I want. There's only one thing I really know—and that is that I love you and want you for ever. For ever, my darling."

It may be that Jill Whitby's nerves could have been stronger, but the idea that their husbands-to-be might at any moment be tried for and convicted of murder would be calculated to make most fiancées feel at least somewhat uncomfortable. So, in the end, Alec himself called on Mr. Low. He found him with Elizabeth, who was knitting.

"I'm very sorry to worry you," he began, but Mr. Low interrupted.

"Not at all. It's very kind of you to return my visit so soon. This is Mr. Morland. My wife."

"How d'you do?" said Elizabeth. "Please sit down."

"No doubt," said Mr. Low, "you've come to tell me what evidence there is against you. That's positively all we want to know."

"We?"

"I have no secrets from my wife. Whether you can trust me or not is one thing. But you can certainly trust my wife as much as me. I have already explained to her that you have not committed the crime of which you may be suspected. So you needn't enlarge on that aspect. It's understood."

"It's very kind of you to take this interest, particularly in view of the way I treated you."

"Not at all. I confess I should like to help the man who had killed Essex—and all the more as you haven't. Too bad to have you convicted of something you haven't done."

"I'm here because of my fiancée really. She can't bear it hanging over us."

"Very natural," said Elizabeth. "I should feel the same."

"Now, just tell me everything that can be proved against you—and I mean everything. No one saw you knock him on the head—because you didn't knock him on the head. No one saw you throw him over the cliff—because you didn't throw him over."

"What am I supposed to say to that?" said Alec.

"I agree it wasn't exactly a question. Let me put it this way. You've seen an inspector who's making inquiries."

"Yes."

"How many times?"

"Twice. Once when he called on me and once when I called to look at the pencil."

"As far as you can tell from what he said, did anyone see Essex knocked on the head or thrown over the cliff?"

"I'm pretty certain no one did. It was a very dark night."

44

"Well—you should know, you were in the neighbourhood, I gather."

"Yes."

"Was the bit of pencil yours—or, I should say, was it like a bit you might have had?"

"It was like."

"Have you the bit it was like?"

"I haven't, as a matter of fact."

"Lost it?"

"I suppose so."

"Not on top of the cliff by any chance?"

"I couldn't say."

"Could anyone except you identify the bit of pencil the police found as being like your bit of pencil?"

"No—I don't think so."

"How long before the murder did you lose it? Or was it before the murder?"

"I don't know. I just hadn't got it when I looked for it—after the inspector had called on me."

"When had you last used it before he called on you?"

"I can't say. The day before, a week before—I just don't know. I didn't use it a great deal."

"Now, the remainder of the evidence against you is that you were seen in Adam Lane by a police officer."

"Yes."

"Is there any other evidence?"

"The police haven't mentioned any."

"But is there any they could find?"

Alec hesitated.

"As you've taken the trouble to come here," said Elizabeth without looking up from her knitting, "you'd better tell us."

"Well," said Alec, "I suppose someone might have seen me in Medlicott."

"When were you there?"

"Just before Essex was killed."

"How long for?"

"A week."

"Where did you stay?"

"At the Lion."

45

"In your own name?"

"Of course."

"Why did you come back to Cunningham on the day Essex was killed?"

"I was following him, as a matter of fact."

"Does anyone know that?"

"My fiancée."

"Anyone else?"

"Not so far as I know."

"The police may have been shadowing Essex too. They ought to have been anyway. They might have seen you go after him."

"I don't think they did. I should have noticed it when we went into the wood."

"So you went into the wood by the cliff, did you?"

Alec said nothing.

"It seems to me," said Mr. Low, "that you ought to have seen who did kill Mr. Essex. You were close enough apparently. However, no doubt you'd hate to give the chap away. At any rate, you feel pretty confident that no one saw him."

"Yes."

"But you may have been seen in Medlicott and can be proved to have stayed at the Lion for a week before Essex was killed."

"Yes."

"And as far as you can tell from what you know and from your talks with the police, that's all the evidence there is against you?"

"As far as I can tell—yes."

"Well—you wouldn't be convicted on that evidence."

"You're sure of that? Can I tell Jill you're quite certain of that? She seems to have a kind of faith in you."

"Yes—you can certainly say that."

"But, of course, it'll still be hanging over our heads."

"That, I'm afraid, is true."

"And Jill will always be wondering if one day someone will come and arrest me."

"Yes—I sympathize," said Mr. Low, "but there's nothing you can do about it. My advice to you is to go home and try to forget it."

"That's easy to say."

"It's not as though there were anything on your conscience."

"No," said Alec, firmly, "nothing's on my conscience."

"Good," said Mr. Low. "Then try to persuade your fiancée to forget it too."

"Pretty hopeless, I'm afraid."

"One other thing. If the police do call on you again, don't tell them anything. Say you're fed up with being interviewed, make any reasonable excuse but don't tell them a thing."

"But suppose they say they want to question me. One's always seeing that so-and-so was detained for questioning."

"They've no right to do that and, if you stand firm, they'll leave you alone. They can only take you to the police station if they arrest you. And they can't arrest you unless they're charging you. Fortunately most criminals have such guilty consciences that they daren't refuse to be questioned. They think it'll be evidence against them. Then they either tell lies or tell the truth. The police don't much mind which they do, so long as they talk. And they nearly always do talk. But don't you talk. Say you've nothing on your conscience and tell them to get out—politely, of course."

Five minutes later, Alec left Mr. and Mrs. Low. As soon as he'd gone, Ambrose said to Elizabeth :

"You know, my dear, I think there's only one thing to be done in this case."

"Go to the police, you mean ?"

"I do."

"Well—now you've started it, you'd better finish it."

"I felt sure you'd agree. How d'you think the Stock Exchange will manage while I'm away ?"

"I'm not at all pleased with you, but I do agree that a thing must be done properly or not at all."

"I hope you'll bear that in mind. I want a son and he's to be a judge."

"I'll compromise. We'll have a daughter and she'll be a judge—the first woman judge—Lady Chief Justice, if you like."

"How horrible."

"Or just in the Court of Appeal—Lady Justice Low."

"Dreadful."

"Well, you couldn't say Lord Justice in the case of a woman, could you? Come to that, you couldn't say Mr. Justice either. It'll have to be Mrs. Justice or Miss Justice."

"I think that's perhaps why they've never made a woman a High Court judge yet."

"Or a County Court judge either. But Her Honour Judge Low doesn't sound so bad."

"All right, we'll make her a County Court judge then. Meantime, you'd better get on with your knitting. I've got a call to make. I shall be some time."

Chief-Inspector Curtis was sitting in his room in the Cunningham police station when he was told that a Mr. Low wanted to see him about the Essex case.

"And what information can you give us?" he asked Mr. Low as soon as he had been shown in. He did not ask it in a friendly voice. He was not in the least anxious to find the man who had killed Essex. He had his duty to do and he would do it, but, like many people, he was delighted that Essex had been removed. Presumably this was an interfering member of the public. Well, if he had any facts to give him, he'd have to go into them, but why couldn't the fellow thank heaven for small mercies and keep quiet about them?

"I have a theory about this case," began Mr. Low, but he got no further before the inspector stood up.

"We don't require to be taught our job, thank you," he said, "you'll find the door behind you."

"No?" said Mr. Low. "I should have thought that the friends and relatives of the girls who were killed by Mr. Essex thought rather differently. No matter. Here's my card if you change your mind."

As Mr. Low left, the inspector snorted: "Theory! Theory!" And, after he had shut the door, he added something to emphasize his opinion of Mr. Low and his theories and of all other people who had theories.

But something happened very soon after Mr. Low had left the inspector's office which resulted in the inspector being compelled to undergo the humiliating experience of calling on Mr. Low to ask his advice.

CHAPTER V

QUESTIONS AND ANSWERS

THE feeling of the public immediately after the death of Gilbert Essex was one of relief. But this was followed by a reaction which was fairly represented by the leading article in the *London Clarion*. This was as follows :

Yesterday this journal received an anonymous letter. Usually we place such communications in the waste-paper basket and disregard them. But not on this occasion. It contained only these words: "The police killed Gilbert Essex." We have ascertained that most of our contemporaries received the same message. We should make it plain at the outset that not for one moment do we accept that theory. On the contrary, we are quite satisfied that nothing of the kind took place. But is it surprising that this false suggestion has been made? How many women Gilbert Essex killed will never be known for certain, but extracts from his diary which have recently been published in some of the more sensation-loving newspapers made it plain that not only had he killed the girl of whose murder he was acquitted, but that the two subsequent murders of women were his work. These last two murders plainly had his signature upon them. The police knew where he lived and yet so little care did they take that these two wretched girls were killed and their murderer left at large. Indeed, he would still be at large if someone had not struck him down. How is it that the police are not able to find the person or persons who killed him? One would have thought that they were watching the murderer so closely that no one could have killed him without their knowing it. Is it surprising then that people are beginning to whisper that the police, unable to obtain by lawful means the necessary evidence against Essex, killed him themselves? Is it possible that they know who did kill him and are deliberately shutting their eyes to the facts? Our police force has in the past been the finest in the world, but these recent events should shock us out of harmful complacency. It is obvious from them that the Force requires overhauling from *top* to bottom. Undoubtedly the person or persons who killed Essex have, in one sense, done a public service, but, great as that may be, no greater disservice can be done than for the rule of law to be abolished or suspended. There can be no exceptions. Once private individuals are permitted to take the law into their own hands, it is the end of civilization as we know it. So start the secret societies which, however laudable their objects may be in the beginning, end by being tyrants and thugs of the worst description. We want no Ku Klux Klan in this country. We should not need it. Let the Police Force be overhauled. Let them begin by showing that they still have some competence and by bringing the *murderer* of Gilbert Essex to justice. Whether he should be hanged will be a matter for the Home Secretary, but justice demands that he should be brought to trial.

It was not long before all the newspapers took up the cry. Again questions were asked in both Houses of Parliament. Faith in the police was gravely shaken. It is true that some of the letters published in the press hailed Essex's murderer as a hero and congratulated the police on not arresting him. For example:

Sir,

Gilbert Essex murdered at least four women. He admitted it. He ought to have been charged with their murders, tried, convicted, and hanged. Had this been done, each member of the public would have been responsible for his execution, as the hangman is only our appointed representative. But suppose he had been charged with these murders and—as he was before—acquitted for lack of evidence. He could, and no doubt would, have gone on to commit more murders. His diary makes this plain. His guilt is admitted. Instead of the slow and expensive process of arresting him and trying him, which involves the employment of large numbers of highly-paid officials, barristers and solicitors and so on—always with the possibility that the trial would be for no purpose and he would again be acquitted—he has been executed at no expense to the public by one or more of its members. I say, sir, that we should be grateful to his executioner. I refuse to call him a murderer. If justice had been done, we—through the hangman—would have executed Essex. He has indeed been saved the anxiety and distress of a trial, but, in the result, nothing has happened to him which ought not to have happened. Why, then, all this fuss? Of course I agree that private execution or vengeance cannot ordinarily be allowed, but the exception proves the rule. The police failed, other women would have been killed, they were saved by the act of a public benefactor. I say—leave him alone.

I am, sir,

Your obedient and normally law-abiding servant,
" Realist".

Card enclosed.

But most people, grateful as they were for the elimination of Essex, took the other view, although many complained that it was outrageous that a private individual had been compelled to take the law into his own hands because of the incompetence of the police. In consequence of the public anxiety and clamour, the Home Secretary said to the chief constable for the district where Essex was killed:

"Look, you really must do something about this. Surely you can find the man."

And the chief constable said to the superintendent:

"Look, you really must do something about this. Why haven't you called in Scotland Yard?"

And the superintendent said to the chief-inspector:

"Look, why did you say you could manage this alone? We ought to have called in the Yard. We'll all be getting the sack, starting with you."

And the chief-inspector replied: "Look, before you call in the Yard, give me twenty-four hours."

"Well," said the superintendent, "I'll give you just that. I'd like to have something to show the CID beyond a stump of pencil which had probably been there for days anyway."

So, twelve hours later, while Elizabeth was knitting and Mr. Low was reading the paper, there came a ring at the bell and Inspector Curtis asked for an interview.

"To be sure," said Mr. Low. "Haven't we met before somewhere, Inspector?"

"In my office, as a matter of fact," said the inspector, not very happily.

"Why, so it was. It was for such a short time that I'd almost forgotten. But something you said, Inspector, stuck in my mind. Now, what was it? Oh yes, of course. Theory. You don't care for theories much, do you? Facts are what you want. Theory!" said Mr. Low in a snort reminiscent of the inspector's.

"Do have a chair, Inspector," said Elizabeth.

"That's very good of you, madam," said the inspector, grateful for a kindly word.

"My wife's knitting, Inspector," said Mr. Low cheerfully.

"Oh—yes," said the inspector uncomfortably.

"That's a fact," went on Mr. Low. "No theories there. Plain hard fact."

"It's associated with theories, though," said Elizabeth. "What's your view, Inspector?"

"About what, madam?" asked the inspector. He was a little out of his depth.

"About babies," put in Mr. Low. "My wife has a theory that husband with strong character, wife with weaker character produces girls and vice versa. Characters about equal chances about equal. Subject, of course, to heredity. Now, I think it's all nonsense. Not heredity, I mean. But any other theory. Apart from heredity, it's just a toss-up. Which view do you favour?"

"I'm afraid I've never considered it."

"Well—as you are here, do," said Mr. Low.

"But, perhaps," said Elizabeth, "the inspector hasn't come all the way from Cunningham to talk about babies."

"I haven't, madam, as a matter of fact."

"What can it be then?" said Mr. Low. "Nothing against me, I hope."

"Oh no, sir."

"That's a relief. Then I'm quite in the dark. I thought it must have been about babies. Now, why should I think that, Inspector?"

"The Inspector's tired," said Elizabeth. "He's had a heavy day."

"Thank you, madam," said the inspector.

"Not at all," said Elizabeth. "It's getting on well, isn't it?" and she held up her knitting.

There was silence for a moment or two. Then the inspector took the plunge.

"You came to see me about the Essex murder, sir," he said.

"Forget it," said Mr. Low. "I was too impetuous. You police must be fed to the teeth with amateurs."

"You said you had a theory, sir," went on the inspector doggedly. "Might I know what it was?"

"Come again, Inspector," said Mr. Low. "I must have misheard you."

"No," said Elizabeth. "He said it. Didn't you, Inspector?"

"I should like to know what your theory is, sir, and what facts you have to support it."

"Well," said Mr. Low, "that's plain enough. D'you know Medlicott?"

"Yes, sir. That's where Essex lived."

"Quite. Why wasn't he being shadowed on the day he was killed?"

"He was under observation, as a matter of fact, sir."

"On that day?"

"May I ask why you're asking these questions, sir?"

"Well—Inspector, if you want my help, you must help me a little too. But I don't want any really confidential matter. The whole world knows he wasn't being watched properly. Why wasn't he?"

"Well—between you and me, sir, he ought to have been, but that was a matter for the Medlicott police at that time. Nothing to do with me. And they just hadn't got a man on at the right time. As a matter of fact, it's a tall order to keep a man under observation twenty-four hours a day all the year round for the rest of his life."

"Well, I see the difficulty. However, that's not my business. D'you know an unlicensed hotel at Medlicott called the Lion?"

"Yes, sir."

"Well, if I were you I should go and look in the visitors' book there."

"Oh?"

"Yes. Then I think you'll know what my theory is. But the name in the visitors' book is a fact."

"And the name is?"

"I'm not going to be had up for slander, Inspector."

"But this is a privileged occasion, sir. You couldn't be."

"So you say, but I'm not taking any chances. All I say is: 'Look in the visitors' book.' There can't be anything slanderous in that. If you draw any conclusions from it, that's up to you."

A sudden thought came to the inspector. "Look, sir," he said, "I know when you came to see me I wasn't very polite. Well, I apologize. But I ought to warn you that if, in order to get your own back you send me on a wild-goose chase, you'll be deliberately wasting public time and money and that's an indictable offence—a public mischief, they call it."

"Well, really, Inspector," said Mr. Low. "This is a bit hick. I call on you and you kick me out of your office. Then you call on me and, instead of kicking you out, I first of all listen to you and my wife chatting about babies, and then I give you some valuable advice. And your retort is to threaten me with prosecution."

"It was a warning, sir, not a threat."

"I fail to see the difference. Don't go to the Lion at Medlicott if you don't want to. You asked for advice and I've given it you. And then you say I'm causing a public mischief. I've a good mind to write to the Press about it."

"I'm sorry, sir," said the inspector, "but how can I tell whether you're just trying to pull my leg or not? After all, maybe I deserve it—and I was just telling you that it's an offence to pull the leg of a police officer that way."

"Well—which way—" began Mr. Low, but Elizabeth intervened with:

"That's enough, dear. The inspector has quite a long way to go."

With some misgivings, the inspector made his way to Medlicott and went to the Lion. He told the proprietor who he was and asked to be allowed to examine the visitors' book.

"I'd like to see your warrant card," said Simon Pudsey, the proprietor.

The inspector produced it.

"I don't like people prying into my affairs," said Mr. Pudsey. "I won't have ordinary inquiry agents doing it, I tell you. No divorce courts for me. But I take it your inquiry isn't for that purpose?"

"No, it isn't."

"All the same, why should I let you see it? Am I bound to do so? Have you a search warrant?"

"I don't want to search the place. I just want to look at the visitors' book."

"Why should I let you?"

"As a public duty. I'm a police officer making inquiries It's your duty to help me. I might even say that if you don't let me look at the book—which I see is there—" and the inspector picked it up, "you'll be obstructing me in the performance of my duties."

"But why should I let you look if I don't want you to? It's a free country still, isn't it, in parts?"

"What harm can it do you? Visitors often look through the book to see if they happen to notice any of their friends having stayed in a place."

"I dare say, but you're not a visitor, and you don't want to look at it for that reason. Anyway, I'm not bound to let a visitor look through it, am I."

"Perhaps not, but I'm going to look at it."

"Can't I order you off my premises?"

"Then I'll look at it outside. Now, don't be silly, old man. I've got my duty to do and I'm going to do it. If you want to complain about it, you can. But don't make a fuss now. You've got my name and you can report me. We don't want a brawl, do we? I shall look at this book and, if you try to take it away, I shall summon assistance. Now, do we understand one another?"

"I never have liked the police," said Mr. Pudsey. "I'm not going to fight you, but I tell you that I don't permit you to look at the book and I order you to put it down and get out. And I'll go to my lawyers about it, if you don't do what I say."

"All right, old man, you go to your lawyers," said the inspector and sat down. "I shan't be long." He started to look through the visitors' book and eventually came to the name of Alec Morland. It gave him a shock. Whatever the truth of the matter was, it was astonishing that Ambrose Low should have known about it. The inspector had never suspected Alec for a moment up till then, but now the piece of pencil and his presence in Adam Lane took on a new significance. But how did Low know all about this? He looked through the visitors' book further, but saw no other names of interest. Low must have been referring to Alec Morland. It was astonishing, and the inspector began to have the greatest respect for his informant, although he could not begin to fathom how he knew that Morland was already very slightly connected with the case. He made a note of the entry and spoke to Mr. Pudsey.

"Thank you very much," he said. "Don't lose this book, will you?"

The inspector left the Lion and went hurriedly back to Cunningham. Mr. Pudsey, who had watched the inspector turning over the pages of the book, tore out all the pages he appeared to have been looking at and burned them. "Interfering busybodies," he said. "Can't call one's home one's own."

As soon as the inspector arrived back at Cunningham, he called on Alec.

"Sorry to trouble you again, sir," he said, "but I'd like to ask you one or two questions."

"I'm sorry," said Alec, "but I'm not prepared to answer them. I've given you all the help I can and I'm rather tired of these interviews."

"I'm very sorry, sir, but I've my duty to do."

"I quite understand that, but I'm not bound to answer your questions and don't propose to do so."

"Well, sir," said the inspector, "of course I can't make you answer them, but I think it's very unwise of you not to do so. If one's a clear conscience, it's much better to help the police."

"I've a perfectly clear conscience, but I've helped you all I'm going to."

"What were you doing in Medlicott, sir, might I ask?" said the inspector.

"That's my business," said Alec, but he was shocked that the inspector knew he had been there. "I haven't to account to the police for all my movements."

"It might save you a lot of trouble if you did, sir. You see, otherwise, unjustified suspicions might fall on you. There was that bit of pencil, you see, sir, you were seen in Adam Lane on the night of the murder, and you were in Medlicott for a week before Essex was murdered. And you left the day he was murdered. Now, if you'd explain the reason for all that, and why you took a stroll in Adam Lane just after you came back from Medlicott, it would be in your own interest, sir, unless, of course, you did kill Essex, and I'm not suggesting for a moment that you did."

"Inspector," said Alec, "I've told you that I'm not prepared to answer any questions and I'm afraid you must take that as final. If, in consequence, you choose to suspect me of the murder, that's your affair. Now, I'm afraid I must ask you to leave me."

The inspector left, extremely puzzled. In his view, Morland's behaviour was not that of an innocent man. Why should he refuse to talk? Alec, on the other hand, was extremely disturbed that the police had discovered about his visit to Medlicott so soon. How could they have discovered it? The only people who knew were Jill and the Lows. None of them could have told the police. Perhaps he had been seen in Medlicott. That must be it. Later he told Jill about it.

"You don't think the Lows could have told them, do you?" she asked.

"I'm sure they wouldn't have. It really would be the last word if they had. They didn't strike me as the kind of people to do that. Did they you?"

"Well, I only saw Low, but I can't think that he'd do such a thing. He seemed really sympathetic. I think you must have been seen by someone."

Later the same day Chief-Inspector Curtis talked to his superintendent.

"That's not bad for twenty-four hours," said the superintendent. "It'll give the Yard something to work on. Meanwhile, you'd better go and see what else your friend Mr. Low can tell you. He sounds a bit psychic, if you ask me."

"He didn't look it," said the inspector. "Nor his wife. She's a beauty, if ever there was one. They're going to have a baby."

"I don't see what that's got to do with it," said the superintendent.

"You would if you met them. They talk about it a good deal."

"Well, you'd better go and hear some more about it then."

The superintendent forwarded a report to Scotland Yard and the inspector called again on Mr. and Mrs. Low, having first telephoned to make an appointment.

"How on earth did you know that Morland stayed at the Lion?" the inspector asked as soon as he could.

"He told me."

"Is he a friend of yours then?"

"Oh—no."

"A casual acquaintance?"

"I've met him once."

"How did he come to tell you he'd been in Medlicott?"

"I don't know exactly. He just mentioned it."

"How did you come to meet him?"

"He came to see me."

"D'you know why?"

"He thought he might be suspected of killing Essex."

"What! D'you mean that?"

"Yes, of course."

"Why didn't you tell me before?"

"Well, Inspector, you didn't seem to have much confidence in me when we first met, so I thought I'd better inspire a little in you. Sorry if I've caused you any unnecessary trouble. Perhaps you'd like a full statement of the interview?"

"I'd be very much obliged, sir."

So Mr. Low gave the inspector a statement and the inspector returned to Cunningham fairly pleased with himself. He still bore no ill-will towards Alec. But, having been told to find the murderer and having had no idea who he was, he felt justified in a little satisfaction at the result of his fortnight's work. It was obvious now that Alec had done it, and the only question was whether they had enough evidence. The superintendent and chief constable were equally pleased. The campaign in the Press had surprised and hurt them and, again, while they bore no malice towards Alec, it was nice to feel that they really were going to be able to show that the police were not as stupid as they were made out.

The next thing the inspector did was to take advantage of a hint which Mr. Low had dropped. In consequence, while Jill was shopping one morning, a police car stopped beside her and she was asked if she'd mind going to the police station. She was very frightened, but she agreed to go. She felt she must. They were all extremely nice to her and offered her a cup of tea and a cigarette, an offer which they usually make to criminals from whom it is hoped to obtain a useful, interesting statement.

"Miss Whitby," said the superintendent, "we're so very sorry to have to trouble you and can well understand that these inquiries must be very distressing for you. I'm sure you understand, though, that we're only doing our duty."

"What is it you want to know?" said Jill.

"Has Mr. Morland ever discussed the Essex case with you?"

Jill did not reply at once. If she answered "No", it would seem obviously untrue. Everyone had discussed the Essex case, even people who had not been visited by police inspectors. If she said "Yes", she would then have to invent the conversation or conversations. She was not used to telling lies and didn't think she would be very good at it. If she just refused to answer, it would look very bad from Alec's point of view. She would have liked simply to burst into tears. But that would have served Alec perhaps even worse than refusing to answer. So she kept control of herself, though she could not decide how to answer the question. The superintendent repeated it. His voice was kind, but he made it plain that he would say it again if necessary.

At last she felt she must say something and she adopted a very normal method of parrying an awkward question.

"Why d'you want to know?"

"Because we're inquiring into the case, madam, and we think you might be able to help." He paused, and then added: "I think perhaps I ought to tell you—and I don't mean to be unkind in saying this—that you have a duty to tell me everything you know."

"A duty?"

"Everyone has, madam. And perhaps I ought to add—and, again, I don't want to appear unkind—that if people tell a police officer something which isn't true, they may render themselves liable to prosecution."

"Well—I haven't told you anything so far, so I can't be prosecuted yet, can I?"

It sounded silly to her as she said it, but she had to speak and a trace of facetiousness seemed easiest before she said it.

"No, you haven't told us anything yet," said the superintendent, and waited.

"I've forgotten what you asked me now," she said nervously.

"I'm sorry," said the superintendent. "Have you discussed the Essex case with Mr. Morland?"

"I suppose everyone's talked about it."

"What has he said about it?"

"In what way?"

"In every way. Has he suggested who might have done it?"

If only I could faint, she thought. Please, please let me faint. Won't the ground open and swallow me up—just temporarily—and then let me be with Alec again, and we'll go away and none of these terrible things will happen. It can only be a dream. It must be. I won't allow it to be anything else. I love him so terribly. And through her thoughts came the voice of the superintendent again: "Has he suggested who might have done it?"

She had to say something. "I suppose everyone's made guesses." She had hardly said it before she realized how stupid it was. People hadn't made guesses. No one had any idea, except Alec and herself—and the police.

"And what guess did Mr. Morland make?"

"I don't remember."

"But you suggested that he made several guesses. Surely you can remember one of them."

"I didn't say he made several guesses."

"Then he only made one—d'you mean? And what was that?"

"I don't feel very well," she said. "Can I go home?"

"Drink this up," said the superintendent, "and you'll feel better," and he handed her a cup. She could hardly hold it. It was as though she had palsy. "He told you he did it, didn't he?" said the superintendent softly but very, very plainly, each word being emphasized. She could not say a word. She would do anything for Alec, die for him, lie for him, do anything for him, but still she couldn't speak. It must be a dream, when the words won't come.

"He did, didn't he?"

Still no answer.

"Well, madam," said the superintendent, "I won't press for an answer today, but when you give evidence you'll have to tell the truth, you know. You'll take an oath."

"Give evidence? When? Why?"

"If there's a case."

"A case ? Is there going to be a case ?"

They did not answer and she had to go on: "Against whom ? For what ?" She was almost sobbing.

"It's not in our hands, madam."

Somehow or other she finished answering their questions. Then she refused the offer of a lift and rushed madly to Alec.

"I as good as told them you did it," she said to him.

"Never mind," he said. "I'll be all right. And I did do it anyway. I'm not going to have you getting into trouble because of me. But how on earth do they know so much ? That's what beats me. It can't be due to the Lows. I couldn't conceive anyone being such a blackguard."

At that moment Mr. Low was telling his wife that he thought he'd require rather more evidence than there was at present.

"Just in case," he said. "You never know. As well to have something up our sleeves."

"I expect you're right," said Elizabeth. "Anyway, it won't do to disagree with you in my present condition. It might give the future Master or Miss Low a complex."

"Make it Master and I'll forgive the complex."

"I'll think it over," said Elizabeth. "Of course, the mischief's done now, whatever it is. You should have thought of it before."

"I'm not sure," said Mr. Low reflectively, "that I should have acted any differently. And now I must leave you, my sweet. I've a call to pay."

CHAPTER VI

A CALL ON COLONEL BRAIN

WHOLLY unaware that he was about to receive a visit from Mr. Low, Colonel Basil French Brain (ex-Indian Army) was talking to Robert Archer, who still adored Alison but had made virtually no progress in his suit.

"My dear boy," he said, "when I was a young man I had a motto. Simple, straight, and to the point. Hug 'em and hope."

"I beg your pardon," said the young man, who had not quite caught the expression.

"Hug 'em and hope," repeated the colonel. "The direct assault. Like all the best plans, simple. It's got me through several campaigns. Not without a scratch here and there, I'll grant you, but, on the whole, with success."

"I don't think I should dare," said the young man. "Alison has such a public-school voice. She'd just stand stiff and motionless and say, 'Don't, Bobbie'."

"Well, of course," said the colonel, "if you've tried it already——"

"Oh, I haven't, Colonel, really. I'm far too terrified. I'm a coward, I suppose. But I just turn to jelly whenever I see her."

"Humph," said the colonel. He was sorry for Bobbie, who seemed a nice young man, but they had more stuffing in his day. Difficult to think of a young man, who daren't kiss a girl, pig-sticking. "But, I suppose," he went on aloud, continuing his thoughts, "pig-sticking isn't really necessary."

"I beg your pardon, Colonel. I don't quite understand."

"Forget it, my dear boy. I was just thinking aloud. You wouldn't understand. Though it was a good sport. Dangerous, mind you, otherwise I'd have been against it. Not fair on the pig. But I used to find the pig had a better chance than I had. That made it all right. At least, I suppose it did. One doesn't think of it at the time. You just pick yourself up and feel glad to find no bones broken. Now, bull-fighting's another matter. I wouldn't have that on any account. It's not English to begin with. I'm all in favour of the bull. Not that I'm against the matador. Dangerous job and he has to earn his living. But it's the crowd. D'you know, my boy, what I'd really enjoy? To see the bull charge into the crowd and toss them to blazes. But then I suppose there might be women in the crowd. No, I wouldn't strike a woman, my boy. That's not English, either. So I suppose we'll have to rule that out. Pity. I'd like to see the bull get a bit of his own back on the one-and-tenpennies. But you were telling me something, my boy. Where was I?"

"We were talking about Alison, Colonel."

"Of course we were. My mind's inclined to run on a bit. Not enough to do, I suppose. Gardening's all right for the old muscles, but not much use to the grey matter. Not referring to my hair, my boy. The stuff underneath. Looks like caviare, I was once told. I'd be a cannibal if it tastes as good. Now, where had I got to?"

"Alison, Colonel."

"Yes, of course. Let me think."

A few moments went by in silence. Then the colonel's brow, which had become furrowed, suddenly cleared. "I know. Can you write, my boy?"

"Not really."

"Dear, dear, that's bad. And you've got a degree. How did you get through your exams? All viva voce, I suppose."

"I mean I'm not a literary chap. I can write ordinarily, if that's what you mean."

"Thank heaven for that," said the colonel. "You had me really worried for the moment. I may be a bit old-fashioned, but, no offence to you, my boy, I find the present generation hard to take. No music, just noise. Where's your 'Merry Widow'? No art, just lines and squiggles. It's not even meant to mean anything. Shouldn't so much mind if it were. I can't draw a pig, but I can have a try. If it's a bad try, it is at least a try. But these chaps don't even try. They boast they're not trying. Abstract, they call it. Well, I say, if thoughts were meant to be drawn, you could see them. Goodness me, the good Lord has given us enough to paint, hasn't he? Trees and fields and people and so forth. But they have to paint thoughts. And what amazes me is, you can never show they're wrong. If no one's ever seen a thought, you can't say it doesn't look like what someone's painted it as, if you follow me. That's what's so exasperating. I got had like that once. Don't much go to see pictures in the ordinary way. Went by mistake. An extraordinarily pretty girl suggested it. I thought she meant a film. However, I made the best of a bad job. She introduced me to one of the artists. 'How d'you like it?' he said and pointed to one of his exhibits. It looked like a very old and decrepit rusk, but it was green. It was called 'Country

Thoughts'. 'D'you want me to be frank?' I asked. 'Not particularly,' he said. 'All right,' I said, 'I will be,' not realizing till afterwards what he'd actually said. 'Well,' I went on, 'the country doesn't look like that. At least, I've never seen it so.' 'It isn't called Country,' he said, 'but Country Thoughts. That's what my thoughts about the country look like.' 'How d'you know?' I asked. 'You've never seen them.' 'Oh yes, I have,' he said. 'Where?' I said. 'There,' he said, and pointed to the picture. Well, what can you do with that, my boy? I muttered something about 'most interesting' and I didn't ask any more questions after that. I should have liked to, though. There was a square wheel. I'm not joking. A square wheel, now I ask you. I suppose if I had asked he'd have said it was 'Thoughts about a wheel'. Well, I suppose you can think a wheel square if you want to, my dear fellow, but you can't use it that way. Except to put in an exhibition. A square wheel! My housekeeper didn't believe me. But then she doesn't always, so that doesn't really signify. Where was I, my dear boy?"

"I think you were going to suggest writing something to Alison, Colonel. It is kind of you to take so much trouble."

Bobbie really meant it. It was such a relief to talk to someone about Alison. He couldn't say anything to his parents. He still remembered what they'd said when he'd said he wanted to become a railway guard. Perhaps not so much what they said as how they'd looked. That was ten years ago, but he could remember the smile still. He never spoke to them about trains again.

"Now, how about this?" said the colonel. "I'm not exactly a literary man either. But I've had to write a few letters in my time—mostly since I left the Army, applying for jobs and so forth. 'Dear—', now I've forgotten her name. Oh, Alison, of course. Then how about 'Dear Alison' for a beginning?"

"I think that will do excellently. I can't thank you enough."

"Not at all, my dear boy. Only too pleased. Been there myself. Now, of course, we might have put 'Dearest Alison', but I'm against that myself. Hug 'em and hope's all right, if she's there. No time to consider it. Why? Because she's there, my dear fellow. And, unless you've made a big mistake, she's going to like it. I did once lose a front tooth though—this one—oh—no, they're all gone now, my dear fellow. I'd forgotten, but that's where it was. Yes, she was a bit of an Amazon, I must say, but that was just a mistake. I went off pig-sticking after that for a time. Look rather a fool going about the battalion without a front tooth. But she was a nice girl. She told me afterwards, it was all a mistake. She was young, you know, and her twin brother had told her what to do if anyone made unwelcome advances. She didn't realize until after she'd done it that they weren't unwelcome. But, of course, I'd gone off pig-sticking by then. So she married a major instead. On the rebound, they call it. Worked out pretty well. He'd lost his teeth years before. She broke his nose once, though. That was a mistake too, but she didn't realize till after she'd let fly. They laugh about it now—at least she does. Now, where was I?"

"You were deciding against 'Dearest Alison'."

"Of course. And then there are even stronger reasons against 'My dearest Alison'. Too patronizing. Some people may think it silly to go through all these motions, but it's the only way if you want to make a good decision. Everyone does the same really—weighs up the pros and cons of the matter, but, unless you do it properly, you get a shoddy decision. Shall I have another kipper? To answer that you've got to do just the same as a general deciding how to fight a battle. First and foremost, what is my object? Do I want a kipper? Well, if I don't, that's the end of it. I don't have it. But suppose I do, will it make me ill? And if it will, will it be worth it? How much do I want the kipper? How ill will it make me? And so on and so forth. You see the point, my dear fellow?"

"You make it very plain, Colonel."

"Thank you, my boy, but it's funny, you know. I failed the Staff College. Still, that's a long time ago. Maybe I've improved."

"I'm sure you have, Colonel."

"Thank you, my boy."

The colonel paused for a moment and then added: "But how can you know, my boy? You've only just met me. If you want to show something's improved, you must know it at at least two stages. That stands to reason, doesn't it, my dear boy?"

"Yes—I see that, Colonel."

"That was quick of you, my boy. As a matter of fact, I only just thought of it myself. Not bad really. You can't say a thing's improved unless you've seen it at at least two stages. Yes—not bad. But I don't like the two 'ats' together. Makes it awkward to say. Particularly if a chap stammers. Might never get off the 'at'. Like a stuck gramophone record. At—at—at— sounds much more like a drum. Ah—the drum and fife. Takes me back a bit."

The colonel then proceeded to go into a quick march round the room, doing his best to imitate both drum and fife and, from time to time, giving or receiving a salute.

"The wrist in line with the fingers. Don't forget that, my boy. Some of these salutes you see nowadays! Hands that look like bent twigs. Don't forget now, the wrist in line with the fingers. So. Battalion present and correct, sir. Thirty-four officers and five hundred and thirty other ranks, sir. Ah—it's a long time since I collected reports."

At that moment the bell rang. It was Mr. Low.

"My dear fellow," said the colonel, "I'm delighted to see you. Come in. I'm afraid we'll have to finish that letter another time, my boy. This is my friend, Mr. Low. And when he calls, it means business. At least I hope so."

"Quite right, Colonel," said Mr. Low. "Business it is."

"Well, I'd better be going, Colonel," said Bobbie.

"I'm so sorry, my boy. But we've got started anyway, if not broken its back. Write out what we've done so far and we'll go on with it tomorrow, if that suits you."

"Thank you very much, Colonel. The same time?"

"That'll do excellently, my boy. And write it out legibly, won't you. The old eyes aren't as good as they were."

As soon as Bobbie left, the colonel turned excitedly to Mr. Low.

"My dear chap, you've come exactly at the right moment. I can't tell you how pleased I am. But how did you find me? I've only been here a few weeks."

"Well, fortunately, you pay your debts, Colonel, and so you left your address behind each time, and I had no trouble in tracing you at all."

"Remarkable, my dear fellow, remarkable. Of course, the Post Office is wonderful the way it finds you. Mark you, I'm not in favour of nationalization, but I believe that if you addressed a letter 'Colonel Basil Brain, England,' it would reach me in the end, unless I was dead. And then, of course, it wouldn't reach me even if it were fully addressed. At least, I don't suppose so. I don't hold much with spooks and so forth, but you can never be sure, can you? I once heard a noise in the night, but it turned out to be nothing, my dear fellow, positively nothing. And then another time I heard one and I said to my housekeeper in the morning: 'Did you hear that noise in the night?' 'I made it,' she said. 'If you will leave your boots in the middle of the landing, what d'you expect?' It all goes to show, my dear chap, doesn't it?"

"It does indeed, Colonel. But it is a lucky coincidence your being at Cunningham—if you hadn't been here, I should have asked you to come."

"Bless my soul, you don't say?"

"I do, Colonel. You'll be able to operate from your own place. Save a lot of trouble."

"Then it isn't gallivanting in the West End this time, I gather?"

"No, I'm afraid not."

"Don't apologize, my dear fellow. I'm game for anything. Now, tell me, is it serious?"

"Very. It's murder."

"That's bad. Called you in too late to prevent it. Poor fellow. Or was it a woman? Poor girl. But how can I tell which to say if you don't tell me, my dear fellow? Poor what shall I say?"

"You won't say poor anything, Colonel. The dead man was Gilbert Essex."

"Goodness me, that scoundrel. Thank heaven he's dead. But where does the murder come in? You can't try him now."

"No, but you can try the man who killed him."

"But why d'you want to? It was a public service, if you ask me."

"I quite agree, Colonel, in a way. But you can't have people taking the law into their hands. What would you have said if an officer in your battalion had given a man a good hiding?"

67

"Wouldn't have happened in my battalion, my dear fellow. Striking a man, never."

"That's what I mean. Even if the man really deserved it, even if he'd been knocking recruits about or something like that, you wouldn't tolerate it, would you?"

"Certainly not, my dear fellow. I did know a chap who shot at one of his bearers. But that was different. He was a general, or became one later, rather."

"So you see the point, Colonel."

"Oh—yes," said the colonel brightly, but then his brow furrowed again. "But, my dear fellow—now I come to think of it, is it quite the same thing?"

"Is what the same thing?"

"Well—my dear chap, you say we wouldn't tolerate striking another rank. Quite right. We wouldn't. But then we don't have corporal punishment in the Army, anyway. But, in your case, the chap who killed Essex is only doing what we'd have done if we'd got hold of him first."

"Yes, that's true, Colonel. But all the same, you can't have private executions. Apart from anything else, it would lend itself to abuse. Somebody might want to execute you, Colonel, quite wrongly, of course."

"Let him try," said the colonel. "Have you seen my armoury? Got licences and all that. All fair and above board. But just let him try. We'd have a shooting match all right. Anyway, what does the fellow want to kill me for? What have I done? Live and let live is my motto. In peace, of course. In war, it's different. Kill or be killed. What's the fellow's name, d'you say? Can't think what he's got against me."

"No one's anything against you, Colonel. I was just giving an example."

"An illustration, I see. Sort of TEWT."

"Sort of what?"

"TEWT, my dear fellow. Tactical exercise without troops. I'll tell you a thing I could never understand. 'W' can stand for 'with' or 'without' just as well, can't it? Then why can't TEWT mean tactical exercise with troops just the same? Beats me. Always has. But what were you saying, my dear chap?"

"This Essex murder. I want some help and you're the man to give it. Are you game?"

"Game, my dear chap? Of course."

"I'm afraid the pay won't be as good as last time."

The colonel's face fell slightly.

"Doesn't matter a bit, my dear fellow. Do it for nothing, if I could afford it. But have to help the old pension out when I can. D'you know what I'm doing at the moment? Gardening. Two bob an hour. What d'you think of that?"

"Capital, Colonel. That'll do admirably. Look, try and get some work at this address."

He gave him Alec's address, and added: "Do it for pretty well nothing, if you like, but try and get in there. I can certainly improve on two bob an hour."

"That's very good of you, my dear chap. Now for my orders. Wait till I get out my notebook."

"You won't need it for the moment, if you get the job, that is. If you don't get it, I'll think up some other way. But have a try. Quick as you can."

"I'll send one of my letters, my dear chap. Take it round by hand."

The same afternoon Alec received the colonel's letter. It read:

Dear Sir,

Passing by your front garden it seemed to me that you could do with some gardening assistance. May I offer my services? I can assure you that the work will be done efficiently and as you like it and I am prepared to offer you a week's trial free of charge. I am a retired officer, living on an Army pension, and I supplement my income in this way. In consequence, I am able to charge you below the current rate. I would not do this if ordinary gardeners had any difficulty in obtaining employment, but, as you know, it is the other way round. I am prepared to work for you for anything from one to five hours a day at any reasonable rate you choose to name and as I said, giving you a free trial for a week.

I hope to be, sir,
Your most obedient servant,
BASIL BRAIN.

"That usually fetches them," the colonel said to Mr. Low before he went to deliver the note. "You see, it provides for every argument that can be raised against me. I can't spoil the garden in a week. Not normally, anyway. I did once dig up a tennis lawn, but that was due to a misunderstanding, and I explained how sorry I was as soon as it was pointed out to me. But the owner cut up rough. Sued me for damages in the County Court. Reported in all the local Press. 'I've no doubt,' said the judge, 'that the defendant'—that was me—'is an excellent gardener, but he's not so good as a witness.' Would have cost a mint of money to have advertised like that in the paper, but I got it for nothing—after paying the damages and costs and so forth, of course."

A few days later Colonel Brain was able to report that he had got his week's trial.

"Splendid," said Mr. Low. "Now, this is all you've got to do. Get on friendly terms with him as quickly as you can. Try and get to the stage when he offers you a drink."

"But, my dear fellow, you know I only touch ginger pop."

"Well—I don't mind. Make it ginger pop. Anything at all."

"Well, that's simple enough, my dear fellow. And then what?"

"While you're having the drink, say 'I'd like to shake the man who killed Gilbert Essex by the hand'. Just that. Now, will you repeat that, please, Colonel?"

"Just say it again first, my dear fellow. The old memory isn't as good as it was."

Mr. Low repeated it.

"Now—please, Colonel."

"I'd like to congratulate the man who killed Gilbert Essex."

"No, Colonel. Shake by the hand."

"Same thing, my dear fellow. Didn't get a degree in English, but assure you it means the same thing. Shake by the hand equals congratulate."

"Yes—I quite understand, Colonel, but it's important that you should say shake by the hand."

"Very well, my dear fellow. Or would pat on the back do as well?"

"No, I'm afraid not."

"Must be shake by the hand?"

"Yes, please."

"Right, my dear fellow. Shake by the hand it shall be."

"Would you mind repeating it then please?"

"I'd like to shake by the hand—shake by the hand—now who on earth was I to congratulate—I mean shake by the hand?"

"The man who killed Gilbert Essex."

"Of course, my dear fellow. The man who killed Gilbert Essex."

"Now, just once more, please, Colonel."

Eventually Colonel Brain had learned his piece to Mr. Low's satisfaction.

"Good," said Mr. Low. "Now, when you leave him after that, shake hands with him."

"Yes, my dear chap. And what next?"

"That's all."

"That isn't much, my dear fellow."

"It's more than you think, Colonel. If you'll just do that, I'll be very grateful. And please report to me as soon as you've done it. The sooner the better."

The same day Mr. Low called on Alec. He found him with Jill.

"Good," he said. "I wanted to see you both. How's everything?"

"It's dreadful," said Jill. "The police have been cross-questioning me."

"Good," said Mr. Low. "I suggested it."

"You *what*!" said Alec.

"I suggested it. Now, keep calm."

"Calm," Jill almost shouted. "Then you're responsible for the police coming after Alec."

"That's right," said Mr. Low. "I am."

The shock was so great that neither Alec nor Jill said anything for a moment.

"Now, what you do next," said Mr. Low, "is this."

CHAPTER VII

PROSECUTION

IN consequence, almost entirely, of Mr. Low's activities, a conference took place at the office of the Director of Public Prosecutions. There had been so much criticism of the police that they did not want to make a mistake. The deputy director presided and the assistant commissioner in charge of the CID and the chief constable for Cunningham, together with Chief-Inspector Curtis, were the most important people present.

"We now have a signed statement from the girl," said the chief constable.

"What girl? The girl who was with Essex?"

"No, I'm sorry. I'll come back to her in a minute. No, I mean from Morland's fiancée. It's quite short, but, if you'll read it, it shows that Morland pretty well confessed to her that he was responsible."

"Pretty well confessed? What were his exact words according to the statement?"

"According to her, he said: 'All right, if you say I did it, I did it. I'm damned glad he's dead anyway. There's nothing on my conscience.'"

"And you'll remember, sir," put in the inspector, "that's what he said to me—about the conscience, I mean."

"Yes," said the deputy director. "We have him in Medlicott for a reason he can't or won't explain, going back to Cunningham on the same evening as Essex goes there, being found near the scene of the murder, and, for what it's worth, the stump of pencil. It's quite a case. Not cast-iron though. '*If* you say I did it, I did it' can be said to be an angry joke or something of that sort. And she only has to add a few words to make a deal of difference. All the same, her evidence does do a lot to tie it up. Very clever of you to get a signed statement from her, Inspector. I'm surprised, though, that she gave you one. Did she take much persuading?"

"Well—she did and she didn't," said the inspector. "It was rather curious. When she first came to the station, she became very upset and I thought I'd better not ask her any more questions. Then a day or two later she turns up of her own accord and says she's prepared to make a statement. And what's more surprising, she made a stronger statement than what she told me originally. I came to the conclusion she must have had a row with her boy friend or something."

"Yes, it's curious. Of course, they may make it up again. In which case, the sooner we get it on the depositions, the better. Now, what about the girl who was with Essex?"

"We've just not been able to trace her. She came into the station the day after Essex was killed. I'm afraid the importance of the matter wasn't appreciated at the time. They took her name and address and she said she'd come in again. The name she gave was Rose Lee. Said she was staying in lodgings. She was, for one night. Of course, she never saw anyone. She told the sergeant she just heard a voice warning her that she was with Essex and telling her to get out of it. Whether or not she'd recognize the voice is anybody's guess and, even if she did, it might not carry much weight."

"Well, you couldn't keep her under lock and key, Inspector. If a witness gives you her name and address, there's not much more you can do about it."

"Thank you, sir. Of course, we're still trying."

"Well, we'll have to assume you don't succeed. Mark you, if you do get her, she not only may be unable to identify Morland's voice, but she might make a witness for the defence and say it wasn't his voice."

"But we know it was him now, sir."

"I dare say you do, but that won't stop a girl whose life's been saved saying it wasn't. Indeed, in view of that possibility, I think it's as much your duty to get her for the defence as for the prosecution. Yes, I think you should ask the defence whether they would like you to appeal to her to come forward. Offer to do it for them or they can do it themselves. This

73

prosecution's got to be thorough, but it's got to be fair. But I'm being a bit premature. We haven't decided even to arrest him yet. I think it'll be best if I get counsel's opinion. I'll go and see Pomeroy at once. Is there anything else to discuss before I go?"

There was not, and the conference broke up after an appointment had been made for the deputy director to see Arnold Pomeroy as soon as possible. A statement of the facts was sent down to him first and a day or two later the deputy director went to see him. Mr. Pomeroy had practised at the Criminal Bar for many years. He was a slightly pompous man of average ability, little imagination, and almost no sense of humour. In spite of these disadvantages, he had done well, and was one of the senior counsel to the Crown in criminal cases. The Director liked him because he was sound and unspectacular. Brilliance is not a particularly desirable quality in prosecuting counsel. The opposition they meet is so often so poor that it would make the scales unfairly weighted if they had the brain and intelligence of a Birkenhead or an Atkin. Fairness and reasonable efficiency are what is required and Pomeroy had these qualities. The absence of a sense of humour was a pity— a controlled sense of humour is nearly always an advantage— but it could not be helped. The deputy director found his lack of humour, coupled with his slight pomposity, rather a bore at times, and he relieved himself by occasionally poking fun at him. There was a fascination in the way it went over Pomeroy's head or round or above or below him, or wherever fun which isn't shared does go.

The conference proceeded as follows.

"I've read these papers," said Pomeroy.

"Good," said the deputy director. "I hoped you would."

"But, of course," said Pomeroy. "Not much point in a conference if I hadn't."

"Very little, I agree, but it's always nice to see you."

"That's very kind of you."

"Not at all. I enjoy these conferences with you. They clear the air. Make me see straight."

"That's most gratifying. Now, where shall we begin?"

"At the beginning, d'you think? First of all, are you satisfied we've got the right man? I've no real doubt myself,

74

but I'd like you to confirm my opinion—that's, of course, if you share it."

"Oh—yes—I don't think there's any doubt of that. It all adds up too well. No, I think you can rest your mind easy on that score. Whether you'll get a conviction is another matter."

"Of course, but I'm glad you're satisfied on the first point. When one's been living with a case even for a short time, one sometimes loses a sense of proportion. That's one of the advantages of having the professions separated. You get an outside view. Slower and more expensive, perhaps, but it makes for a higher standard."

"I quite agree with you. Yes, I've read these papers most carefully, and it's obviously Morland."

"Good. Now, what about the chances? First of all, is there enough evidence to put him on trial?"

"Oh—yes, I think so. It's all circumstantial, except for the admission to Miss Whitby, but you'd certainly get a committal on that evidence. At the trial everything will depend on two things. First, how Miss Whitby stands cross-examination and, secondly, how Morland gives evidence and how he stands cross-examination. He's got to explain his visit to Medlicott and his return on the day of the murder. He's also got to explain why he wouldn't give Inspector Curtis any explanation of his visit. But, of course, he'll have plenty of time to think up his story, and there'll be a lot of sympathy with him. The jury will let him off, if they can."

"Well—what d'you think? Shall we go ahead now or see if there's any more evidence to be got? Rose Lee, for instance?"

"Oh—no, I shouldn't wait for her. You ought to try to find her though. As you pointed out in the instructions—either for the prosecution or the defence. I don't think myself she'll carry much weight, but you can never tell. No, I should fire ahead."

"I think I'd like you just to put your opinion in writing, if you will. Just a short one will do. But there's been so much noise about this Essex affair, we ought to be covered."

"Certainly I will. But, if you're really worried about it, why don't you go to the Attorney?"

"Well, I will, if you think we should."

"Well, I don't, quite candidly. He couldn't say any more than I have. But, of course, it's always a safeguard if you've got his backing. Arnold Pomeroy might be wrong. So might the Attorney. It doesn't matter if he is. It does if I am. But, on this occasion, I'm not. There's nothing to be wrong about. Anybody would say there's a case. Anyone would say it's not a certainty. So it's up to you. Murder never is a certainty anyway. Look at the Orkney case, for instance. Everyone knew the man was guilty, but the jury let him off."

"You prosecuted in that case, didn't you?"

"Yes, I was led by Hislop."

"Pity they didn't leave it to you."

"Oh I don't know. I expect the result would have been the same."

"I'm not so sure. Your cross-examination, if you don't mind my saying so, would have been more effective."

The deputy director was being malicious, though, of course, Pomeroy did not notice it. There is almost a standard form of cross-examination of the prisoner by regular prosecuting counsel. Half of it usually consists in putting the Crown's case over again and asking the prisoner if he says the witnesses are liars. Pomeroy was no exception to the rule and was no match at all for an intelligent witness who had something of a case. He would even be reduced to saying sometimes: "So that's what you say, is it?" with a look at the jury to indicate that presumably they, as intelligent persons, will not believe the witness. The use of this unfair comment has been accepted for years, though it is not a genuine question. The witness is not meant to answer "Yes, it is." It is simply a comment by counsel at a stage in the case when he is not entitled to comment. When a judge is sitting alone, e.g. in some civil cases, it is more a retreat than an attack and is most often used when counsel has received an answer which doesn't suit his case and cannot think of any helpful further question on the point. No judge sitting alone would dream of rebuking counsel for the comment, because it is the judge's mind which has to be affected and it is not in the least affected. But when there is a jury, it is conceivable that the impact on the jury of the witness's answer—which is the evidence—is deflected by counsel's comment, and it ought not to be.

The deputy director and Pomeroy continued chatting for a short time. It was as a result of their conference that a few days later the newspapers contained a statement that "the police hope shortly to make an arrest in connection with the death of Gilbert Essex." A week later Alec was arrested and charged with the murder of Essex. He was brought up before the Cunningham justices. Evidence of arrest was given and the superintendent asked for a week's remand. This was granted. The following week a representative from the Director of Public Prosecutions appeared and asked for a further remand of a week.

"I shall be in a position to open the case next week," he said.

Alec was accordingly again remanded for a week.

During that week subpœnas were issued and served on the various witnesses, including Jill. Within a day or two of the subpœna being served upon her, the following letter was received by the Director of Public Prosecutions' office.

It was sent by solicitors acting for Jill.

We are acting for Mrs. Alec Morland—formerly Miss Jill Whitby —upon whom a subpoena in her maiden name has been served. Our client is not prepared to give evidence against her husband and we shall be glad to know that, in the circumstances, she may be relieved from attending upon her subpoena. Our client was married by special licence at the Norminster Register Office on the 14th instant.

An immediate conference was arranged between the deputy director and Pomeroy.

"This is a nice kettle of fish," said the deputy director. "I suppose we ought to have thought of the possibility. What do we do now?"

"We'll just have to go ahead," said Pomeroy, "and see what the Bench think of the case. There's probably enough to obtain a committal, but, in any event, there's nothing else you can do. In view of the public disquiet, I should imagine that you'd prefer to go on now. If the Bench throw it out, that's their responsibility."

"I think perhaps I'll get you to prosecute. I was going to

leave it to Dalby, but, as it's a bit tricky, I think I'll get you to come down."

"Certainly," said Pomeroy, "I think perhaps you're right."

Accordingly, on the day fixed for the hearing, Pomeroy opened the case before the magistrates. "May it please your Worships," he said, "I appear to prosecute in this case on behalf of the Crown and my learned friend Mr. Duffield appears for the prisoner."

Duffield had been averse to accepting the brief in the first instance. "I don't like appearing for friends," he said, "unless it's only a trivial matter. One may let oneself become too biased. I will never do it in the ordinary way. If you absolutely press me, I don't feel I can refuse, but I'd prefer you to go to someone else."

But they had pressed him and reluctantly he consented to appear.

"The charge against the prisoner—who, I should say at once, is a man of excellent character—is that he murdered Gilbert Essex on the 15th June last. It is no good pretending that everyone does not know who Gilbert Essex is—or perhaps I should say was. Nor is it any part of my duty to dispute that it appears unquestionable that the death of Essex has been a great relief to the community. I accept that he was a murderer who ought to have been hanged. But I do not have to remind your Worships that no private person can be allowed to take the law into his own hands, however laudable his motives may be. The only question you have to consider is whether the prosecution make out a *prima facie* case that the prisoner murdered this man, and, when you have heard the evidence, I shall invite you to say that there is such a case and that the prisoner ought to stand his trial in due course. It is perhaps right that I should say at the outset that the case for the prosecution is not as strong as it was anticipated it would be when the prisoner was arrested. This is because one witness whom it was intended to call is no longer available as a witness for the Crown."

At that point Duffield got up.

"I thought the object of opening the case to your Worships

78

was to tell the Court what the evidence for the Crown is going to be, not what it is not going to be."

"I wish my learned friend would not interrupt," said Pomeroy.

"I am sorry for having interrupted, and I am even more sorry for the necessity," said Duffield. "I will only say now that, much as I shall regret it, I shall continue to interrupt as often as my learned friend makes unfair statements in his opening. I am indeed surprised that he has started so soon. Usually he gets more warmed up first."

"That is an outrageous thing to say," said Pomeroy, "and I am amazed at my learned friend saying it."

"No more than I am at my friend referring to the non-availability of a witness. He knows quite well why the witness is not available and I cannot think of any reason for his mentioning it except unfair prejudice."

"Really!" said Pomeroy. "This is too bad. My learned friend is attacking me personally and I must ask the Bench for protection. I have been practising now for over fifteen years and no one has ever made such a suggestion before."

"I hope you haven't given them cause," said Duffield.

"Really, gentlemen," said the chairman. "It would be much more helpful to the Bench if you would get on with the case. If you think it profitable, you can continue your argument at some convenient place outside the court when we have risen."

"I'm sorry, your Worships," said Pomeroy, "but I am not used to this sort of treatment."

"It has stopped now," said the chairman. "Please continue your opening."

"If your Worship pleases," said Pomeroy.

He then proceeded to outline to the Bench the evidence which he was proposing to call. When he had finished, the chairman said: "Is that all the evidence you are going to call?"

"In this Court, yes, your Worship."

"Does that evidence, if given, do more than raise a case of suspicion against the accused? Strong suspicion, if you like, but suspicion rather than proof?"

"In my submission, it will raise a *prima facie* case against the accused. It will then be for him to rebut the evidence. I quite agree that it is circumstantial but, as has been said many times, circumstantial evidence may be the best. If you call a man who says he's seen a crime committed, he may be telling a lie or genuinely mistaken. But if there are a number of circumstances, each of which is, as it were, a sign-post and each one of those signposts points in exactly the same direction, eventually the time comes when one must say that that is the right direction."

"Quite so, Mr. Pomeroy, quite so," said the chairman. "But how many signposts do you need before that stage is reached? One isn't enough, is it?"

"Certainly not, your Worship."

"Nor two, nor, I should say, three, except in a most exceptional case. How many do you say you have here?"

"Certainly more than three, your Worship."

"And which do you say are the most important?"

"They are all important, your Worship, but I should say that the most important are the prisoner's visit to Medlicott and his return on the day of the murder, coupled with his refusal to explain that visit and his call on Mr. Ambrose Low."

"Suspicion, if you like," said the chairman. "But I went to Medlicott about that time myself. Am I to come under suspicion just because I leave the place on the day on which someone is murdered?"

"Well, your Worship, he didn't just leave the place. He went to within a very short distance of the place where the man was found dead. I suggest that your Worship didn't do that. Moreover, I do not imagine your Worship, if questioned by a police officer, would have objected to giving the reason for your visit. Nor did your Worship go to someone and say that you thought you might be suspected of the murder."

"That's quite true, Mr. Pomeroy, and you're quite right that I would certainly have given an explanation to the police. I dare say all my colleagues would have done so too. But, after all, we are magistrates. Some people don't like being questioned by the police. Some people do get unnecessarily frightened of the police, and do silly things which create an appearance of guilt where in fact there is none."

Pomeroy continued to debate the matter with the chairman for some little time and then started to call his evidence.

That evening Mr. Low talking to Elizabeth said:

"You know, I'm afraid there's a good chance of their throwing this out. They oughtn't to, but they might. I think we'd better start Operation Brain, don't you?"

"I suppose so," said Elizabeth, "but I'll be glad when it's all over. I don't think Miss Low approves either."

"Master Low," said Mr. Low firmly, "will understand when he's older. Now, I must go and wind up the colonel."

CHAPTER VIII

OPERATION BRAIN

"So far, so good," Colonel Brain was saying to Bobbie. "We've agreed on 'Dear Alison'. Now, shall we begin gently or with a short sharp shock? What d'you think, my dear boy?"

"How d'you mean, Colonel?"

"Well, a gentle beginning would be: 'I so much enjoyed having tea with you last Sunday' or as the case might be. A shock would be: 'I adore you.' We've got to make up our minds about that first, haven't we? Oh dear, there's the bell."

It was Mr. Low, and Bobbie had to be sent off again, with his letter no further advanced than the first two words.

"Now, just tell me the conversation between you, Colonel."

"Well, my dear fellow, I did exactly as you said. 'I'd like to shake hands with the fellow who killed Gilbert Essex', I said. He murmured something which I didn't quite catch. Then he asked me about the potatoes and the subject dropped. And when I left, I didn't forget, my dear fellow. I shook him warmly by the hand."

"Good for you, Colonel," said Mr. Low. "Now, I'd like to go into it in a little more detail, if you don't mind."

"Certainly, my dear chap. With a microscope, if you like."

"Your memory isn't as good as it was, is it, Colonel?"

"Sound as a bell, sir."

"Your memory, I said, Colonel, not your heart."

"Good as it ever was."

"Was it always good?"

"As good as the next man's."

"Well—what was his memory like?"

"I didn't ask him, my dear fellow. Who d'you mean anyway?"

"The man you mentioned, Colonel."

"But I didn't mention anyone, my dear fellow."

"Oh yes, you did, Colonel. That's what I mean really. As one gets older, one's memory is inclined to play one tricks. I find it myself."

"Do you really, my dear fellow, you don't say?"

"I certainly do. It's the same with all of us. Now, tell me, Colonel, what did you say to him when he said: 'I'll give you the opportunity'?"

The colonel looked puzzled. "I'll give you the opportunity?" he repeated.

"That's right," said Mr. Low. "Say it again."

"Say what again?"

"I'll give you the opportunity."

"Just those words?"

"Yes."

"Now?"

"Yes, please."

"You want me to say them to you?"

"That's it, Colonel. D'you mind?"

"No, of course I don't, my dear fellow, but I can't quite see the point, if I may say so, but no offence, I hope."

"None at all, Colonel. There are a lot of things one doesn't understand at the time."

"By Jove, my dear chap, there are. Which reminds me, there was a thing I wanted to ask you——"

"Would later on do?" interrupted Mr. Low. "Would you mind repeating the words I asked you to say now?"

"Certainly, my dear fellow, certainly."

The colonel paused.

"Now, let me see—let me see—confound it, I can't think what they were. Gone clean out of my head."

"Just what I was saying, Colonel. That's what happens to all of us."

" 'Pon my word, you're right, my dear chap, 'pon my word, I believe you are. Now, what was it you wanted me to say?"

"Just to repeat what Morland said to you—you remember—'I'll give you the opportunity'."

"Of course, my dear fellow, 'I'll give you the opportunity', that was it, 'I'll give you the opportunity'. But——" and the colonel's brow became furrowed. "He didn't say that to me, my dear fellow. That's what you said."

"Oh—no, Colonel, you just told me yourself. How could I know if you hadn't told me? I wasn't there, was I?"

"No—you weren't there, my dear chap, but——"

"You just told me as plainly as you could, Colonel, what happened between you. Shall I repeat what you said?"

"I wish you would, my dear fellow. 'Fraid you're right about the old memory and all that. Bad, though. Didn't think it would happen to me."

"What you said was this, Colonel. You said that in talking to Morland you said: 'I'd like to shake the man who killed Gilbert Essex by the hand.' "

"That's right. That's what you'd told me to say."

"And then he replied: 'I'll give you the opportunity.' "

"Is that what he said then? He murmured something, but I couldn't hear it."

"But you did hear it, Colonel. You just told me quite plainly."

"Did I really, my dear fellow?"

"You did indeed. And how right you were, Colonel. Because he's been arrested for murder now."

"Yes, that's true, my dear chap. Can't help having a sneaking regard for the fellow all the same. What was it you say he said?"

"No—it's you who said he said it."

"Well—what do you say I said he said?"

"I'll give you the opportunity."

"Are you quite sure, my dear fellow?"

"Positive."

"Well—you're usually right, my dear chap. So I suppose you are this time."

"Have you ever known me wrong, Colonel?"

"Can't say that I have, my dear chap."

"Well, then, just tell me what he said."

" 'I'll give you the opportunity.' "

"Why did he say that?"

"Couldn't tell you, my dear fellow."

"Oh yes, you can. It was because you'd said you'd like to shake the man who killed Gilbert Essex by the hand. Don't you remember saying that?"

"Of course I do, my dear fellow."

"Well, what did he reply?"

" 'I'll give you the opportunity', I suppose. If he said it at all, he must have said it then. Wouldn't have made sense anywhere else. Not when we were talking about potatoes, anyway."

"Well, let's have the conversation again just as it took place, Colonel."

"You tell me first, my dear fellow."

"Certainly, but it's only what you told me yourself, Colonel. I couldn't know otherwise, could I?" After a further half-hour's intensive indoctrination, Colonel Brain was convinced that he had said to Alec:

"I'd like to shake the man who killed Gilbert Essex by the hand," and that Alec had replied: "I'll give you the opportunity," and that, a moment later, he had shaken him warmly by the hand.

As soon as Mr. Low was satisfied that the colonel was sufficiently indoctrinated, he telephoned Inspector Curtis.

"I suggest," he said, "that you call on Colonel Brain at Leach Cottage and ask him if he had a conversation with Morland about Essex."

"Thank you, sir," said the inspector, and went to see Colonel Brain immediately.

As Duffield was going home a day or two later, he was stopped by Mr. Low.

"There's a surprise witness going to be called in the Morland case," he said. "I shouldn't cross-examine him much at the Magistrates' Court, if I were you."

"What's all this about?" said Duffield.

"Just a suggestion, that's all," said Mr. Low.

"What business is it of yours?"

"An interest in justice, nothing more. The same as we all have, I hope."

"You're a witness for the prosecution, aren't you?"

"That's right."

"Who suggested your speaking to me?"

"No one."

"Who knows that you have?"

"No one."

"Well, I warn you, I shan't treat this conversation in confidence. I shall tell anyone I think fit about it."

"Do so, by all means," said Mr. Low. "I merely gave you a piece of information and a piece of advice. You may do what you like about them."

Duffield was extremely puzzled by this conversation. But he remembered Mr. Low's part in the Prout case. The man was not a fool. What he was after he had no idea. Was it to help the prosecution or the defence? In any event, he, Duffield, had left himself complete freedom of action in the matter and had not been guilty of the least impropriety. He decided to postpone a decision until he saw what happened. Perhaps it was all nonsense and no surprise witness would be called. When a case of this kind was being heard, all sorts of ideas got around. Probably that was it. It would not be the first time he had heard unfounded rumours in similar circumstances. Though he had never received them from a similar source. Oh yes, he had though. Once a man in the train had given him a piece of information about a case he was in. Complete nonsense, of course. So was this—probably. But, at the next hearing, he had something of a shock when Pomeroy said:

"I did not mention the next witness in my opening to your Worships. I was not aware that he would be available. Colonel Brain, please."

So he was right, after all, thought Duffield. Now, what am

I to do? I wonder what he was after when he told me not to cross-examine him too much at the Magistrates' Court. Well, I'll have to make up my mind soon. I wonder what he's going to say.

Alec, too, was surprised at Colonel Brain being called, but he could not think what the reason was. He was not unduly alarmed, however, as nothing had happened in Colonel Brain's presence which could possibly affect the matter. But a few minutes later, when he heard the colonel's evidence, he was amazed and furious. So the colonel had been planted on him. It was disgraceful. Even more enraging was the fact that everything the colonel said was true, except the one vital interpolated sentence, "I'll give you the opportunity" and the timing of the handshake.

"With your Worships' permission, I will reserve my cross-examination of this witness until next week."

"Certainly," said the chairman, after discussing the matter with the other justices. "It has been a surprise to us as well as to you. It is only fair to warn you, too, that this evidence—unless it is completely destroyed—appears to me and my colleagues to put a different complexion on the case."

"I am very much obliged to your Worship for that intimation," said Duffield.

Later that evening Mr. Low called on Jill. "It's all going very nicely," he said.

"What d'you mean?" she said miserably. "It was all going very nicely until this new bit of evidence turned up."

"It's just what we wanted," he said. "They'd have thrown it out otherwise."

"I believe you're really on the side of the police. You're just pretending to help us in order to do us down."

"I suppose it does look a bit like that," said Mr. Low. "Let me explain."

CHAPTER IX

CROSS-EXAMINATION

WHILE Mr. Low was explaining matters to Jill, Duffield was considering whether to accept the advice given to him or not. Eventually he came to the conclusion that he must act just as he would have done had Mr. Low not spoken to him. When an important witness gives evidence at the Magistrates' Court, defending counsel is afforded an opportunity for what may be called trying him out. He can try every kind of cross-examination upon him, he can find out his weak spots, if any, he can see whether he is a man who is likely to lose his temper, whether he is a man who is likely to give way, if pressed, and so on. On the other hand, such cross-examination is a two-edged weapon, as it prepares the witness in advance, and, if counsel merely repeats his previous cross-examination when the prisoner is on trial, the witness is well prepared to deal with each question. Accordingly, the proper method to adopt varies with each case and each witness, and, for the most part, it is experience only which tells the advocate what course to adopt. He has also to remember that if he refrains from putting really important questions to the witness, the judge may think that they are afterthoughts and therefore untrue, and, in some cases, the jury may also be led to this conclusion. Although, therefore, the advantages of being able to cross-examine each witness before the trial are considerable, the experienced advocate takes the greatest care to ensure that he does not convert his advantage into a disadvantage. Even then, he may make an error of judgment or, even if his judgment is right, things may go wrong. Duffield, having considered all the circumstances, decided that he must test the colonel's evidence pretty severely to see if it was likely to withstand his assault at the trial. In consequence, the cross-examination of Colonel Brain at the Magistrates' Court a week later went as follows:

Duffield: Are you quite sure of everything you've told us, Colonel?

Colonel Brain: Sir, I have taken an oath to tell the truth.

Duffield: So does every witness, Colonel, but none the less they make mistakes sometimes.

Colonel Brain: Do they indeed, sir? Your experience is greater than mine, no doubt, but, to my mind, the truth is the truth, whatever you may say. You cannot make black white or white black.

Duffield: But you can think it is, can't you, Colonel?

Colonel Brain: Never, sir, unless one is colour blind.

Duffield: But—just to test your evidence for a moment—are you really saying that you have never heard of an honest witness making a mistake?

Colonel Brain: If you'd mention the name of the witness, sir, I would try to answer your question.

Duffield: No special witness, any witness.

Colonel Brain: In what case, sir?

Duffield: In any case, Colonel.

Colonel Brain: But I may not know about the case, sir.

Duffield: I am referring to cases you know about, Colonel.

Colonel Brain: Thank you, sir. That makes it much easier. Then would you just tell me which particular case you have in mind?

Duffield: Really, Colonel! Do you not understand plain English?

Colonel Brain: I understand and speak it, sir, and no other. It was good enough for my father and it's good enough for me. But legal English is another matter, sir. Can't make head or tail of it.

The Chairman: I don't want to interrupt you, Mr. Duffield, but is it really necessary to ask this witness if honest people make mistakes? We know they do.

Duffield: I'm much obliged to your Worship. I appreciate that, but I thought a few questions on the subject might, to some extent, give a clue to the witness's mentality. If your Worships will bear with me, I will ask the question just once more.

Colonel Brain: As often as you like, as far as I am concerned, sir. I am here to speak the truth.

Duffield: Accepting that for the moment, may you not have made a mistake?

Colonel Brain: In what respect, sir?

Duffield: In any respect.

Colonel Brain: I'm sorry, sir, but, unless you tell me the particular mistake you say I've made, I can't possibly correct it.

Duffield: Then you agree you may have made a mistake?

Colonel Brain: Certainly not, sir. I agree to no such thing.

Duffield: Then what would there be to correct?

Colonel Brain: That's what I should like to know, sir.

Duffield: Oh—well. Now, Colonel, why did you say to the accused that you would like to shake the hand of the person who killed Gilbert Essex?

Colonel Brain: Because that's what I felt, sir. A fine fellow, if I may say so. The right stuff.

Duffield: You approve of murder then, Colonel?

Colonel Brain: Certainly not, sir. I may add, sir, that I am in favour of retaining the death penalty. No second chances, I say.

The Chairman: The Bench would be glad if you'd confine your remarks to answering the questions, Colonel Brain.

Colonel Brain: I'm sorry, sir, I thought I was. Must I just answer Yes or No?

The Chairman: As far as possible, yes, please.

Colonel Brain: Very good, sir.

Duffield: You realize this man is about to be on trial for his life?

Colonel Brain: Yes, sir.

Duffield: And that if you make a mistake, it might have terrible consequences?

Colonel Brain: Yes, sir.

Duffield: Why did you want to shake by the hand a man who had committed murder and who apparently, in your view, ought to be executed?

Colonel Brain: No, sir.

Duffield: No what?

Colonel Brain: Well, I was told to say "Yes" or "No", and "Yes" didn't make sense.

Duffield: What sense does "No" make?

Colonel Brain: I'm afraid I hadn't thought of that, sir. (*Turning to the chairman*) I'm afraid I'm finding this very difficult, sir.

The Chairman: I only said that you should say "Yes" or "No" when possible. Obviously, if the question can't be answered by a plain "Yes" or "No", you must say something else.

Colonel Brain: Thank you, sir. That will be a great help. I understand you want my views on the death penalty, sir. Now I think—

Duffield: I don't want anything of the kind, Colonel. I want to know what prompted you to want to shake a murderer by the hand.

Colonel Brain: I never wanted anything of the sort.

Duffield: But you've just told us you wanted to shake the hand of the man who killed Gilbert Essex.

Colonel Brain: A fine fellow, sir.

Duffield: But if he killed him, it was murder and he was a murderer.

Colonel Brain: It isn't murder to kill a rat or a poisonous snake.

Duffield: But he was a man, not a rat.

Colonel Brain: You will permit me to differ, sir, on that point.

Duffield: Then you would have killed him yourself, Colonel?

Colonel Brain: Certainly not, sir. Can't take the law into one's own hands.

Duffield: But the man who killed Gilbert Essex did take the law into his own hands.

Colonel Brain: That's why I say he was a fine fellow, sir.

Duffield: But he killed a man.

Colonel Brain: A rat, sir, not a man.

The Chairman: You seem to be back where you started, Mr. Duffield.

Duffield: If I could get started at all, your Worship, I should feel I had achieved something. Now, Colonel Brain, my client quite agrees that you did make the statement about wanting to shake the man who killed Gilbert Essex by the hand.

Colonel Brain: Of course he does, sir, because I said it.

Duffield: But I suggest to you that he said nothing whatever about giving you the opportunity.

Colonel Brain: What is the question, sir?

Duffield: Is it true that he said he would give you the opportunity?

Colonel Brain: Absolutely, sir.

Duffield: I suggest to you that it is quite untrue.

Colonel Brain: What is the question, sir?

Duffield: Is that last answer of yours not quite untrue?

Colonel Brain (after a pause): Yes, sir.

Duffield: You agree with me then?

Colonel Brain: I agree with you, sir.

The Chairman: To what are you intending to agree, Colonel Brain?

Colonel Brain: That my last answer—well—at least it isn't my last answer now—but what was my last answer at one time, if you follow me, sir, is not quite untrue. It isn't untrue at all. Putting it another way, sir, it's true, if that makes it easier for you. These double negatives are always rather difficult. At least I find them so, sir.

Duffield: I put it to you that it is quite untrue.

Colonel Brain: What is the question, sir?

Duffield: Really, Colonel Brain, I don't know if you're intending to be difficult or if you can't help it, but surely you can understand what I'm putting to you.

Colonel Brain: I'm here to answer questions, sir, and doing my best to do so. I'm not allowed to do anything except answer questions.

Duffield: When I put something to you or suggest something to you, it is really a question.

Colonel Brain: What is the question, sir?

Duffield: I'm just telling you something in the hope that you can understand it. Do you understand it?

Colonel Brain: Understand what, sir?

Duffield: Understand that if I put or suggest something to you, I am really asking you a question.

Colonel Brain: What question, sir?

Duffield: Any question.

Colonel Brain: About what, sir?

Duffield: About anything. (*He waits for an answer.*) Well, Colonel?

Colonel Brain: It all sounds very vague, sir. I'm afraid you've tied me up and all that. You want me to answer you any question about anything. Well, I will if I can, sir. But, if it's a subject I know nothing about, I may not be able to. I'll do my best, sir.

The Chairman: Mr. Duffield, this method of cross-examination by putting something to a witness is no doubt very familiar to most of us and perfectly proper, but, strictly, I suppose the colonel is right. You should put it in the form of a question.

Duffield: I'm bound to put my case to the witness.

The Chairman: Of course, Mr. Duffield, and, if I may say so, I certainly—and I expect my colleagues on the Bench also—admire your persistence and care in the face of considerable difficulties. But really this "suggesting to" and "putting to"—hallowed by antiquity as it is—is really not asking a question, unless it is followed by "Do you agree?" or some similar phrase. Of course, from the advocate's point of view, it's more effective not to add those words, but, strictly speaking, I suppose they should be added. Colonel Brain is surely right in saying that he is there to answer questions.

Duffield: If you please, your Worship. Colonel Brain, I put it to you that the accused did not say "I'll give you the opportunity". Do you agree?

Colonel Brain: I do not, sir.

Duffield: Are you quite sure he said it?

Colonel Brain: Quite sure, sir.

Duffield: Why are you so sure?

Colonel Brain: Because he said it, sir, and I heard him. And may I add something, sir?

Duffield: What is it?

Colonel Brain: You were not there, sir, and I was.

Duffield continued to cross-examine the colonel, but the witness remained quite definite on the main point of his evidence. When he had finished, Pomeroy asked him one question in re-examination.

"Have you any doubt," he asked, "about the conversation of which you have spoken?"

"None of any kind, sir," said the colonel. "I am as certain of it as I am certain that I stand here."

The next witness called by the prosecution was the landlord of the Lion at Medlicott. After he had been sworn and asked the necessary formal questions, he was asked if he recognized the accused.

"I may have seen him," he said. "I don't know. I see a lot of people."

"Can you say if he stayed at your hotel between the ninth and fifteenth of June last?"

"I've no idea. He may have. He may not. A lot of people stay there. I can't remember everyone."

"Will you produce the visitors' book, please?" The witness

produced it and it was handed to Pomeroy. After a few in-effectual efforts to find the relevant entry, he asked for the book to be handed to the witness.

"Would you mind finding the entry of Alec Morland, please?"

"It's not here," said the witness.

Pomeroy spoke to the representative from the Director of Public Prosecutions in an undertone.

"But I was told that Inspector Curtis had seen it."

"Yes, he saw it. He told me quite definitely."

"Send the book out to him. Let him find it then." Pomeroy then addressed the Bench.

"If your Worships will forgive me. I'm having the right page ascertained from Inspector Curtis so that the witness can identify it. I apologize for the delay."

The book was taken out to the inspector, who became ex-tremely angry when he found that the page in question was missing. He sent a message to Pomeroy telling him it had been torn out. Pomeroy then spoke to the witness.

"Just take the book again, please. Have some pages been torn out?"

"That's right."

"Who tore them out?"

"I did."

"May I ask why?"

"That's my business. It's my book and if I choose to tear out pages, that's no concern of anyone else."

"Don't you have to keep a visitors' registration book?"

"I do."

"Well, where is it?"

"Here."

"But this isn't complete."

"It was once. I registered everyone who came. I haven't got to keep the book for ever, have I? Any other questions?"

"Mr. Pudsey," said the chairman, "your attitude is a most unsatisfactory one. You are under a public duty to answer questions and you must answer them properly. Moreover, if it is the case that you have destroyed evidence, it may be a serious matter for you."

"Who's talking about destroying evidence? No one told me it was evidence. I can do what I like with my own book, can't I?"

"When did you tear out the pages?" asked Pomeroy.

"Some time ago."

"After Inspector Curtis paid you a visit or before?"

"After."

"Why?"

"Because I don't see why I should have policemen prying into my affairs. I've done nothing wrong. Why should I have him asking me questions, looking at my books and refusing to go when I tell him to?"

"At any rate," said Pomeroy, "the pages for the dates between the ninth and fifteenth of June last no longer exist?"

"That's right."

"In that event, your Worship, I shall have to call secondary evidence to prove the entry in question. But your Worships will also remember that, as I told the Bench in opening, the accused did not dispute that he had been in Medlicott when the inspector spoke to him about it."

"Is my learned friend calling evidence or making speeches?" asked Duffield.

A little while later the Court adjourned for lunch. Pomeroy and Duffield left together.

"Where's the best place to have a bite?" asked Pomeroy.

"I'll take you," said Duffield. "What about a quick one first?"

"I never do when I'm working," said Pomeroy.

"Very wise," said Duffield. "Hope you won't mind watching me."

"Not at all, old boy."

While Pomeroy and Duffield were relaxing in 'The Bull', Alec and Jill were allowed to lunch together in a room in the Magistrates' Court. It was, of course, locked and guarded by a policeman.

"I really don't know what to think, darling," said Jill. "And even if what Low says is right, if he makes a mistake, I don't know what might not happen."

"You mustn't worry too much, darling," said Alec, "though I know how difficult it is. But I think he is a hundred per cent on our side. Of course, I didn't at first and, even later on, until he explained, I wasn't at all sure of him. But he is right in saying that, unless I'm tried and acquitted, we'd have it hanging over our heads all our lives. And that would be the case even if the magistrates dismissed the charge. I've got to be tried and acquitted. Then we'll be all right for ever."

"It sounds wonderful, darling. But I wish it would happen quickly."

"I know. It's worse for you than for me. But, as for Low, his conduct doesn't make sense unless he's for us. He tells you to give a statement against me and then to marry me quietly so that, with luck, the police will think you're available as a witness when they arrest me. Then, when the case looks as though it may be dismissed, his Colonel Brain appears on the scene to make enough evidence to secure a committal."

"He might have asked us if we'd take the risk first. He's not taking any."

"Well, I believe him when he says he deliberately took the decision for us. After all, it would be very difficult for me to say I didn't want the magistrates to throw out the case. What he's doing—at least, so he says—is to force me to trial for my own benefit. I believe him. And I believe him, too, when he says I'll be acquitted."

"But if you're not! It's easy for him. He hasn't to stand in the dock. He's under no risk of being sentenced—sentenced—oh—darling, I can't bear it, I just can't bear to think of it."

He comforted her as best he could. When she was calmer he said:

"You know, I keep on remembering what he said about the appendix. 'Much better to have a grumbling appendix out', he said. 'I'm the surgeon, and I'm going to take it out whether you like it or not. You'll thank me in the end.' "

"So we shall when you're free. But it's waiting till then that's so difficult. But I will try. I'm only making things more difficult for you like this."

That night Mr. Low confided to Elizabeth that he was a little worried about Colonel Brain.

"I warned Duffield not to cross-examine him. As a matter of fact, I was frightened he'd break him down too soon, but, instead of that, from what I've heard, he's made him a bit too strong. It'd be pretty awful if the jury convicted him because of old Brain's evidence. I may have to disindoctrinate him. I must say I thought that Duffield would do that all right at the Assizes. But I'm not so sure now."

"You sound worried," said Elizabeth.

"Well, I am a bit. You see, no one's going to think the colonel's a liar. An old fool, yes, but a liar, no. Of course, no jury will want to convict Morland, but if they have too strong a sense of duty—well, they mustn't anyway."

"I hope," said Elizabeth, "you're not going to tell me that having got this wretched young man and his wife into all this trouble, you're going to make a mess of it."

"Well—he started it by killing the fellow."

"But they'd never have prosecuted but for you."

"Well, it was the only way of giving them a clean start, the only way they could live the rest of their lives without fear. And, my sweet, you agreed with me."

"I did, but I confess I trusted you not to make a mess of things."

"I haven't yet—and don't propose to do so. I'm just a bit worried, that's all. I expect it'll be all right."

"And if it isn't?"

"Well, he won't be hanged, I'm sure."

"Just a life sentence, you think? That's jolly for a newly married couple."

"He'd be let out after a year or two."

"You're not Home Secretary, you know. There is still a death penalty. And to show that people can't be allowed to take the law into their own hands, he might make an example of him. You're not saying that's impossible, are you?"

"Not impossible. But unlikely. Anyway, it won't happen. He'll get off."

"You hope."

"I'll make sure he does."

"How? You see it isn't as though you could suddenly say it was all your fault and clear the whole thing up, because, unfortunately, he happens to be guilty. So for you to make a clean breast of it is worse than useless."

"I've no intention of making a clean breast of it. I've had worse difficulties than this and got rid of them."

"But those were your own."

"True enough, but I'm just as interested in these as though they were mine."

"So you ought to be. You made most of them."

"With your full agreement."

"Now we're back to that again. What I want to know is what are you going to do?"

"For the moment—nothing. See what the evidence amounts to when he's committed. And then perhaps pay a call on the colonel."

But the worry which Mr. Low felt at the time he was speaking to Elizabeth was as nothing to what he felt shortly afterwards, in consequence of circumstances over which he had no control whatever. Then, indeed, he wished that he had never interfered.

CHAPTER X

ANOTHER EXECUTION

"The Court will take time to consider its judgment," said the Lord Chief Justice, presiding over the Court of Criminal Appeal. He was referring to the case of The Queen against Brown, which was an appeal against a conviction for murder. William Brown had been convicted of the murder of a married woman named Alice Hastings. The evidence against him had been mainly circumstantial. Among other things, he was alleged to have said: "If I can't have her, no one shall", and, shortly afterwards, her dead body had been found. She had been stabbed to death. It was a sordid story. Mrs. Hastings had left her husband for William Brown, but Mr. Hastings had not taken her desertion and preference for William Brown with equanimity. He brought an action against Brown for enticement and, having recovered damages, he levied execution on Brown's furniture and effects. Partly in consequence of this action, Brown lost his job and Mrs. Hastings found her standard of living seriously deteriorating. She started to have rows with Brown on the subject and eventually threatened to return to her husband. This, said the prosecution, was too much for Brown. He had lost everything for Alice and he was not going to lose her too, or, if he could not keep her, no one else should have her. It was one of those cases where the parties concerned were not far removed from the lower animals and were nothing like as pleasant as most dogs and most horses and some cats. Now, although the whole neighbourhood, and Mr. Hastings in particular, were convinced of Brown's guilt, the prosecution had, by no means, a cast-iron case against him. They had a strong case, but that was all. He was tried at the Assizes and the jury, after a short retirement, found him guilty. The judge sentenced him to death. In due course he appealed to the Court of Criminal Appeal. After the appeal had been in progress for only a short time, it became plain that the judges were not happy about the case.

"I agree," said the Lord Chief Justice during the hearing, "that there was ample evidence on which the jury could convict but are you saying that no reasonable jury could have acquitted?"

"I suppose I can't go as far as that, my Lord."

"Well, then, if the direction of Mr. Justice Plank was wrong, how can you sustain this conviction? Of course, if that direction was wrong, what ought to happen in the interests of justice is that the appellant should be tried again before a fresh jury. But, unfortunately, this Court has no power to order a new trial. This is probably another example of a case which shows how unfortunate it is that Parliament still withholds from us that power."

Eventually, after careful argument on both sides, the Court reserved judgment. It was delivered a week later. With some regret, the Court felt it had no alternative but to quash the conviction. The appellant was set free, and he walked into the nearest public house to celebrate his release. He had, however, only just raised the tankard to his lips, when he died suddenly. The cause of his death was much the same as that of Mrs. Hastings. He was stabbed to death. This time there was no doubt whatever as to who had done it. Indeed, Mr. Hastings never sought to deny his guilt. On the contrary, he alleged it. "If the something judges think I'm going to let him get away with it, they're something well mistaken. If he's the right to kill my wife, I've the right to kill him. You can do what you something like about it. I'm something well fed up."

So Hastings was duly tried, convicted, and sentenced to death. He did not appeal, and the doctors pronounced him sane. His execution date was fixed. And then the trouble began. A petition was launched for his reprieve. Unsuccessful attempts were made to raise the matter in the House of Commons, the inflexible rule being that a debate on the subject can only take place after the Home Secretary has made his decision and it has been carried out. If that decision is in favour of clemency, then the man or woman concerned may live to read about the debate, but, if a reprieve is not recommended, the debate will be of no interest whatever to the condemned person. Although some people think it undesirable that a man's execution should be discussed in the House of Commons while he is lying under sentence of death, others think that it is possibly a little unsatisfactory that, whether or not a man shall live or die, can only be debated after he is dead. Still, the House of Commons can change this rule if it wishes. Apparently at present it does not desire to do so. Nor does it desire that the responsibility for recommending a reprieve or not should rest on more than one man's shoulders. A jury, after all, are twelve. The judge has no discretion in the matter. The Home Secretary can seek advice, but the decision is his and his alone. The difficulties and dangers involved in having more than one person to decide the matter are obvious, but, as long as there is a death penalty, there is a body of opinion which would prefer a permanent responsible tribunal to consider the matter. Whether that tribunal would decide by a majority or whether its decision would have to be unanimous is one of the difficulties which would have to be faced if such a tribunal were appointed. However, the case of Hastings had to be decided by the Home Secretary, and he found it a very difficult decision to make. It was as plain as it could be that Brown was a murderer. Indeed, after his death a letter was found which virtually clinched the matter. He had killed Hastings' wife and he, himself, was killed by Hastings almost immediately after his release by the Court of Criminal Appeal. Might not a man in these circumstances be said to have been robbed of normal self-control to such an extent as to justify clemency being exercised in his favour? There was the murderer of his wife about to drink to his acquittal. The law had failed. Hastings had lost his wife and now he had lost even the satisfaction of seeing the law exact its penalty from her murderer. Very difficult for a man to bear, particularly a man of the low mentality of Hastings. On the other hand, although the Home Secretary was not a lawyer, he appreciated that Brown had been acquitted by a court of law and that it would be the negation of law if private vengeance were given the least encouragement. Knowing that whichever course he took many people would disagree with him, he was extremely worried. He was by no means impervious to other people's criticism, and he was not in fact the right man to have to make a decision of this kind. Such decisions require cold, clear thinking, unaffected by sentiment but not inhuman. They can be properly influenced by other people's views, but not by other people's pressure. A judge who constantly worries about his decisions is not usually a good judge. One unfortunate and over-conscientious judge actually died as a result of the worry the work caused him. The Home Secretary in the present case would have been likely to suffer the same fate if he had had many of such cases. He lay awake at night, trying to come to a conclusion. His wife was sympathetic, and she missed some sleep too.

"You poor dear," she said, "it must be dreadful for you."

"It can't be very pleasant for Mr. Hastings," replied her husband.

"At any rate," said his wife, "he hasn't any decision to make. It will be all done for him."

"I know," said the Home Secretary, "but the question is —what is to be done for him?"

Eventually, after an earnest and honest endeavour to come to a right conclusion—as though there could be a right conclusion in such a matter: what the Home Secretary subconsciously meant by right was what most people would think right—the Home Secretary recommended a reprieve. And then the storm broke. The editorial in the *London Clarion* fairly represented a substantial body of responsible public opinion. Part of it was as follows:

We have never looked upon the Home Secretary as a strong man, but we did at least think he had ordinary courage and some appreciation of his duties, however unpleasant. Who now will be safe from the man or woman who seeks private vengeance? What is the point of having a law at all? Is the Home Secretary seeking to abolish the death penalty without the sanction of Parliament? It is difficult to think otherwise. There have, of course, been cases in the past where public opinion has been divided, but this was a plain case of deliberate murder. "If the law will not kill him, I will," said Hastings. And he did. What is the death penalty for, if it is not to apply to such a case? Granted that Brown, too, should have been hanged, it has long been a principle of our law that it is better that a hundred guilty men should be acquitted than that one innocent man should be convicted. Through the meshes of that net—deliberately constructed so that no innocent person should be caught—some guilty men must swim to freedom. Human justice cannot be perfect, and we pride ourselves on letting off the guilty so that in no circumstances may the innocent be punished. But what is the use of this principle if, as soon as a man—guilty or innocent— is acquitted, the hand of the assassin is allowed to strike him down? We are back to the law of the jungle. The Prime Minister should show his disapproval of the Home Secretary's act by calling for his resignation. Or the Home Secretary should bow to public opinion, acknowledge his terrible mistake, and resign of his own accord. One way or another, he cannot remain any longer in the Government. Or, if he does, the public will show their opinion of this matter at the next election.

Unfortunately for the Home Secretary, the Government had only a small majority and an election was not far off. It was not that the particular decision to recommend a reprieve would have been likely to influence the voters, but at such a time political nerves are not in the best state. Question after question was asked in the House and the Home Secretary received a buffeting, even from members of his own party, that he could not forget. Eventually, without the least pressure being put on him by the Prime Minister or his own party, he tendered his resignation. He felt he was embarrassing the Government.

He had a faint hope that it would be refused. It was—just, but in such terms that he felt compelled to offer it again, and he knew that this time it would be accepted.

My dear George, wrote the Prime Minister,

It is with the greatest regret that I received your second letter. I had hoped than I should have succeeded in changing your resolve. No man has worked harder than you or performed more useful service to the Government and to the Country, and your resignation will be a great blow to us and to me personally. At the same time, I do not think it would be right of me to embarrass you by a further refusal to accept your resignation, and I must reluctantly, therefore, yield to your decision. You have my warmest thanks for all you have done in the past.

Yours most sincerely.

The absence from the letter of any reference to possible further help the Home Secretary might be able to give in another capacity was not accidental. A new Home Secretary was appointed. He, also, was not a lawyer, but he was what could be called a strong man. He was also a firm believer in capital punishment.

It is not surprising, therefore, that these events were a considerable shock to Mr. Low. When he had started his well-meant interference, he had felt quite sure that, if the worst came to the worst, Alec Morland would only serve a prison sentence. But now there was a very different picture. Although Alec's killing of Essex was not from motives of private vengeance and although by killing him there is hardly any doubt but that he saved at least one life, and possibly several lives, nevertheless there was an unpleasant similarity between the two cases. In each a man had been acquitted by a court of law and a private individual had killed him. And the new Home Secretary was just the kind of man to say importantly that the rule of law must be observed and that it was sometimes necessary to be severe in order to uphold a principle.

Alec, too, who was allowed to see the papers in prison, realized the possible implications of the Brown-Hastings case. He tried not to discuss the matter with Jill when he saw her, as her anxiety was becoming more acute, but it was impossible not to do so.

"Of course you'll get off, darling," she said one day, "but do you think this Hastings case will make any difference?"

"Of course it won't," he said, "but, even if it did, it won't affect me. I'm going to be acquitted."

"Yes—I know, darling, but I wish it would happen. It seems so terribly long, and the thought of the jury considering their verdict seems so awful. One never thinks about it when it's someone else involved."

"I know," he said. "It is a long time and it will be a strain for us both, but we'll come through in the end and then Low's right, we'll have happiness and peace for ever."

"Oh, darling—it sounds so wonderful. Please make it happen, and quickly. Oh—please, quickly."

"There'll be no delaying tactics on my side," he said. He spoke with some feeling. With the present shortage of staff and buildings, it is inevitable that prisoners awaiting trial in custody must be harshly treated. They are, of course, not treated as convicted persons but their conditions of living are—for innocent people—quite deplorable. In the case of murder and some other serious crimes and in certain other cases it is impossible for bail to be granted, but it is obviously desirable that, as all accused people are presumed innocent until they are found guilty, they should not be punished more than is absolutely necessary. Deprivation of liberty is a very severe punishment, but, in certain cases, it is essential in the public interest. It is not, however, in the public interest that the accused should be as uncomfortable as he is while awaiting trial. The manpower shortage and the acute lack of sufficient prison accommodation at present makes impossible any serious improvement of the position of a person awaiting trial in custody, but it is to be hoped that the improvement of his position does find a place on the list of things to be done when the more urgent problems have been solved.

Alec was intensely worried about Jill. From being a normal, healthy and strong-minded young woman, she was becoming almost helpless. The strain was too great. It was not altogether surprising. She could think of nothing else but Alec and his trial. Over and over again in her mind, asleep and awake, she visualized it. She saw Alec in the dock, heard the judge sum up, heard the jury's verdict. Sometimes it was Guilty, sometimes Not Guilty, sometimes they disagreed. She heard witnesses examined and cross-examined, she saw Alec in the witness box, watched and heard while the judge intervened with a searching question from time to time. But what she heard most often when she visualized Alec giving evidence was the question asked him by his own counsel. Did you kill Gilbert Essex? When she was awake he always said "No", quietly and calmly and as she wanted him to do. But when she dreamed, he made every kind of terrible answer. "What should I want to kill him for?" he said on one of these occasions. And, at other times, "Yes, of course", or "I don't really remember, it's such a long time ago", or "I'm not quite sure. Would you mind repeating the question?" Even when he said "No", it was not always satisfactory. In one dream she often had, he said and repeated, "No, no, no, no", to the tune of the first movement of Beethoven's fifth symphony. In another he said it to the tune of the funeral march in the Eroica. She heard the judge pass sentence of death sometimes in quite fantastic terms, and sometimes even when the jury had acquitted him. Once the judge said that, in view of the fact that he was a married man, he would send him to prison for a hundred and fifty years instead. "And you may go with him too", he said, with a kindly smile to Jill just before she woke up. On that occasion she woke up smiling, for a fraction of a second gloriously happy that she would have a hundred and fifty years with her darling. What did it matter where? But, as with all such dreams, the happiness faded almost immediately. Occasionally she found herself in the dock with him, holding hands, or sometimes trying to hold hands but just not able to reach. "Is that your wife with you?" asked the judge during one of these dreams. "Yes, my Lord", said Alec. "I think she'd better come and sit next to me", said his Lordship and she went and sat next to the judge. She stroked his wig and he purred and became a cat. But he could still speak. "Did you say milky or guilty?" he asked the jury. She remembered thinking in her dream how she and Alec would laugh together over this when she woke up, for she knew she was dreaming. But, when she did wake up, the laughter was gone, It was just another day, another day nearer his trial.

That she did not actually break down was a tribute to her

strength and to the help of her friends. And at last the day of the trial came, the day she longed for and the day she feared, but the day that had to come before they could ever know happiness again.

CHAPTER XI

THE CASE FOR THE CROWN

"MEMBERS of the jury," said Pomeroy, who was conducting the case for the Crown with a junior, "I do not need to remind you that the only question which you have to try in this case is whether the prisoner killed Gilbert Essex or not. You must put out of your minds, as far as you can, that Gilbert Essex once stood in that very dock and that a jury of twelve said he was innocent when he was, as we now know, guilty. It may not, though, perhaps be out of place to remind you that, after his acquittal, he went on to commit other murders. In the same way, *if* this accused is guilty, I repeat *if* he is guilty and you acquit him, how many more murders do you think may be committed by people taking the law into their own hands ?"

At this stage the judge, Mr. Justice Pantin, one of the oldest Queen's Bench judges, intervened.

"I'm sorry to interrupt you, Mr. Pomeroy, but do you not think that it would be of more assistance to the jury if in your opening you dealt with the facts the prosecution intend to try to prove, rather than with the consequences of conviction or acquittal in this or any other case? If you feel it necessary to mention such matters, I should have thought that your closing address would be the more appropriate place in which to deal with them."

"If your Lordship pleases," said Pomeroy, "but, in view of the publicity attached to this case, I thought it desirable to say a few words by way of introduction."

"Very well," said the judge, "you have said them. Perhaps now you would open the case for the prosecution."

So Pomeroy opened the facts to the jury at some length. He told them of the finding of Essex's body, of the piece of pencil on the cliff, of the prisoner's visit to Medlicott, of his refusal to account for this visit, of his calling on Mr. Low, and of his statement to Colonel Brain. Then he went on:

"There is one witness I am unable to call, although every effort has been made to trace her. These efforts have been made as much for the benefit of the defence as for the prosecution. As I have told you before, it is no part of the duty of the prosecution to seek at all costs to secure the conviction of a prisoner. On the contrary, it is our duty to place all the material facts before you, even those in favour of the prisoner—if there are any. The witness to whom I refer is a girl called Rose Lee."

At that stage Duffield got up.

"I do apologize for interrupting my learned friend," he said, "but do I understand that, if Rose Lee could be found, he would call her as a witness for the prosecution?"

"Certainly," said Pomeroy, rather crossly. He had been annoyed by the judge's intervention and he was not pleased at being interrupted again. In consequence, he said "Certainly" perhaps rather more quickly than he had intended.

"Well, in that case," said Duffield, "I should tell my friend at once that she's outside the court. We have managed to find her."

This was the first sensation in a case which was attracting even more public attention than the trial of Gilbert Essex.

Pomeroy was rather taken aback by Duffield's announcement. "I wish my learned friend had told me before," he said.

"I only learned of it this morning," said Duffield, "and I was not aware that the Crown was prepared to call her as a witness in any event. No doubt, of course, those instructing my learned friend will wish to interview her."

"This is all very interesting," said the judge, "but I thought that Mr. Pomeroy was opening his case to the jury. If either of you has any application to make to me, please make it in a regular way. Otherwise, kindly conduct any discussions of this kind between yourselves. It is most unsettling for the jury to have this cross-talk between counsel in the middle of an opening."

"Well, my Lord," said Duffield, "in these circumstances I have an application to make to your Lordship. Might the trial be adjourned to enable what I might call a voice identification parade to take place?"

"This is really most inconvenient," said the judge. "Surely that could take place during the luncheon adjournment or between today and tomorrow? This case is bound to take some little time."

"If your Lordship pleases," said Duffield. He was quite satisfied to have obtained so easily a promise by the prosecution to call the girl. Mr. Low, at the cost of many visits to many public houses and the following of many false trails, had eventually found a girl called Rose Lee, who said she was the girl in question. Before risking an identification parade, he had tried her with various types of voice and was at last satisfied that the one point she would make plain was that it was an uncultured voice which had said to her "The man you are with is Gilbert Essex". No one could have said that Alec's voice was uncultured.

"Now, let's get on," said the judge.

So Pomeroy continued and eventually began to call the evidence. Duffield did not cross-examine much until Inspector Curtis was called, but he rose as soon as Pomeroy had finished examining the inspector in chief.

"Inspector," he said, "how many times altogether did you have an interview with the prisoner before you arrested him?"

"Four, sir."

"And it was at the last interview that he refused to answer any further questions?"

"Yes, sir."

"Up till then he had been perfectly frank and open about the matter and given you all the assistance for which you asked?"

"Yes, sir."

"He is a man of the highest possible character?"

"Yes, sir."

"With a fine war record and nothing against him of any kind?"

"Yes, sir."

"Did it occur to you that he might be rather tired of being interviewed?"

"He didn't show any signs of it until the fourth interview."

"Maybe not. But I suppose you'll agree, Inspector, that people do sometimes get tired of being questioned by the police."

"Some people don't like it at all, sir."

"And the accused said he didn't?"

"That is so, sir."

"Had you any reason to disbelieve him?"

"No, sir, I believed him."

"When you first went to see him, you had in fact no suspicion in your own mind that he was in any way responsible for the death of Essex?"

"None at all, sir."

"And when that interview was over, you still had no such suspicion?"

"No, sir."

"Did he seem in the least upset or worried by your calling on him?"

"Not as far as I could tell, sir."

"Nor at any of the other interviews until the last?"

"No, sir, I can't say that he did."

"And, apart from refusing to answer any more questions at the last interview, did his attitude or behaviour indicate any apprehension on his part?"

"Not apart from his refusal, sir."

"Did that refusal surprise you, Inspector?"

"Yes, it did, sir."

"That was because up to that time he had always co-operated with you to the full?"

"Yes, sir."

"Inspector, I don't mean this offensively, but d'you think perhaps he'd got tired of you by then?"

"I couldn't say, sir."

"He might have?"

"I couldn't say, sir."

"Well, I suppose it's more a matter of comment. I'll leave it at that. Now, another matter, Inspector. I take it you've been in charge of this case from the start?"

"Yes, sir, under the superintendent."

"What kind of a watch was being kept on Gilbert Essex?"

"As far as possible, he was kept under observation, sir."

"But I take it that he was not seen or followed on his last journey from his home to Cunningham?"

"No, sir."

"Anyone might have followed him?"

"Quite, sir."

"Or no one?"

"Yes, sir."

"I'm trying to see what evidence there is against my client, Inspector. He stayed at Medlicott?"

"Yes—sir."

"I suppose a good many people stay there."

"Quite, sir."

"And he went back to his home at Cunningham?"

"Yes, sir."

"Nothing strange in that, Inspector?"

"Not by itself, sir."

"He is seen on the night of the murder in a lane not far from the cliff?"

"Yes, sir."

"Nothing strange in that, Inspector?"

"Not by itself, sir."

"A lot of people must have been within the same radius of the cliff as the prisoner?"

"I expect so, sir."

"And a piece of pencil which he could have owned is found at the place where Essex was thrown over?"

"Quite, sir."

"Hundreds of people might have owned it?"

"Yes, sir."

"Thousands?"

"Very likely, sir."

"Even hundreds of thousands?"

"I expect so, sir."

"And, apart from Colonel Brain's evidence, that's the case against him, isn't it?"

"Not altogether, sir."

"Oh—no, I forgot—he got tired of talking to you, Inspector."

And Duffield sat down, having made quite a pretty little

speech to the jury in the guise of cross-examination. The trial continued until lunch time and, during the luncheon adjournment, arrangements were made for Rose Lee to have an opportunity of identifying or failing to identify the voice which had warned her. True to his promise, Pomeroy called her as a witness for the prosecution after lunch, but before he did so, he said:

"My Lord, my next witness is the girl Rose Lee. I should make it plain to your Lordship and the jury that I am only calling her because I undertook to do so and not because I rely upon her evidence."

Duffield did not complain at this statement. He felt entirely satisfied that the prosecution called the girl. She went into the witness box and, after giving formal evidence as to her name and various addresses, she was asked to deal with her meeting with Essex.

"I was having a drink in the Crown," she said, "when a man came in and sat next to me."

"Were you alone?"

"Yes."

"Go on."

"Well—he got talking to me and he seemed a nice gentleman. He ordered me several drinks and then suggested that we should go for a walk together."

"I take it you had not recognized who he was."

"Oh—no, sir. He seemed a quiet gentleman. Refined, if you know what I mean."

"What happened?"

"Well—we went for a walk and he suggested going into the wood and, as he seemed all right, I said I would. So we walked into the wood. After we'd been a little way, he said he was tired and suggested sitting down. He seemed a very nice gentleman. So we sat down."

"Yes, Miss Lee, and what happened then?"

"Well—suddenly I heard a voice say something. It was dark and I couldn't see anyone."

"What did the voice say?"

"Well, as far as I can remember, it told me to run away."

"Is that all it said? Run away?"

"Oh—no, it said more than that."

"Try and remember what else it said."

"Well—it said something about my being with Gilbert Essex and to run away."

"What did you do?"

"I didn't know what to do at first, but the voice said it again. So I got up and ran. But I didn't know if it was true. He seemed a nice gentleman."

"Could you recognize the voice if you heard it again?"

"Oh—I don't think so. It was just a voice."

"Yes, but voices are different. Was it a man's or a woman's voice?"

"Oh—a man's."

"Was it a rough voice?"

"I wouldn't know, sir. It was just a voice, a man's voice."

"About an hour ago were you taken to a room and did you hear some voices?"

"Yes."

"Saying something like what you heard the voice in the wood say?"

"Yes."

"Were any of those voices like the one you heard?"

"I couldn't say, sir."

"While you were listening to those voices, did you think that any of them was like the one you heard on the night in question?"

"Not exactly, sir, but it's so difficult to tell, and it's some time ago now, sir."

"Since you were with the nice gentleman, you mean?"

"Yes, sir."

"Very well, Miss Lee. Thank you. No, don't go away. Mr. Duffield may want to ask you some questions."

"Very few," said Duffield as he rose.

"Do you remember when you were listening to the voices during the adjournment that you heard a voice which was called Voice B?"

"I don't remember the numbers, sir."

"Well—never mind about the letters. Do you remember this gentleman sitting in front of me coming up to you with another gentleman and asking you if that was the voice?"

"They came each time, sir."

"Quite. And did you tell them each time whether you thought it was the voice or like the voice or nothing like the voice?"

"Yes, sir."

"And do you remember saying once or twice, 'That wasn't it, at least I don't think so'?"

"Yes, sir."

"When you said that, was that your honest opinion? That it was not the voice in question?"

"Yes, sir."

"Thank you."

The first witness on the following day was Colonel Brain. His evidence in examination in chief was similar to what he had said before the magistrates. Early in his cross-examination, Duffield suggested to him that the words "I'll give you the opportunity" had never been said.

"Now, it's funny you should say that," said the colonel.

"Why is it funny?"

"Because a man said that to me yesterday."

"What man said what to you yesterday?" asked the judge, in a somewhat stern voice.

"It was all perfectly friendly, my Lord. I hope I haven't said anything I shouldn't."

"What man said what to you yesterday?" repeated the judge.

"I was in the garden having a nap, my Lord, as a matter of fact," said the colonel.

"I dare say you were, but who came to you and said what?"

"I'd had rather a heavy day," said the colonel.

The judge tapped his desk impatiently with a pencil. "Colonel Brain," he said, "will you kindly answer the question?"

"Certainly, my Lord," said the colonel and waited.

"Well?" said the judge, after a moment's pause.

Colonel Brain smiled cheerfully towards him.

"Will you kindly answer the question, Colonel. You can hear, can't you?"

"Very well, my Lord. As a matter of fact, I had a test the other day and——"

111

"Be quiet, sir," said the judge loudly.

"I'm sorry, my Lord," said the colonel, and relapsed into a crestfallen silence. The silence continued for a time. It was broken by the judge.

"Colonel Brain, I don't know if you're being intentionally perverse, but, in case you are, I should warn you that I shall have no hesitation in sending you to prison."

"Prison, my Lord?" said the colonel unhappily. "I can't think what I do, my Lord. That's what the Lord Chief Justice said to me when I gave evidence. I find it terribly difficult. I'm only trying to help, my Lord. First your Lordship asks me if I'm deaf and, when I start to explain, your Lordship tells me to be quiet. Then, when I keep quiet, you say I must go to prison."

"My Lord," intervened Duffield, "if you will allow me to say so, I think the witness has some difficulty in appreciating what is required of him. I had considerable difficulty myself with him in the Magistrates' Court. As he is a witness for the prosecution, I think I can properly say that I don't myself suggest that he is trying to be obstructive."

"That's very civil of you, sir," said the colonel, beaming towards Duffield.

"Be quiet, sir," said the judge, and the smile left the colonel's face.

"Perhaps I'd better go," he said. "I don't seem to be doing much good here."

"You will kindly stay in the witness box until I say you may leave and you will answer the questions which are put to you sensibly and properly. Is that understood?"

"Yes, my Lord."

"Very well, then."

Again there was a silence.

"Colonel Brain," said the judge, controlling himself as well as he could, but obviously with some difficulty, "you are being asked a perfectly simple question. Will you kindly answer it?"

"Of course, my Lord," said the colonel. "I understand that's what I'm here for."

"I'm glad you realize that at last," said the judge.

112

"Oh—my Lord," said the colonel, "I've realized it all the time."

"Very well then. Answer the question."

"Yes, my Lord—when I know what it is."

The judge said nothing for several seconds, while he looked keenly at the witness.

"Are you telling me," he said eventually, "that you don't know what the question is?"

"Not in advance, my Lord. D'you mean you want me to guess what it is, my Lord?"

"I mean nothing of the kind. Do you mean to tell me you were a colonel in the Army?"

"A lieutenant-colonel, my Lord. If I'd known that was the question, I'd have answered a long time ago."

"It was not the question."

"I'm sorry, my Lord. Shouldn't I have answered it then?"

"Well," said the judge, "I suppose it is quite a long time ago now since you were asked the question."

"About the Army, my Lord?"

"No—not about the Army," the judge almost shouted. He paused for a moment and went on: "Now, let's be quite calm and collected about this——"

"Of course, my Lord."

"Be quiet, sir," said the judge.

"I'm sorry, my Lord, I thought you were going to ask me a question."

"I am about to do so."

"Will I go to prison if I answer it, my Lord?"

"Colonel Brain, will you kindly say nothing until I have asked you the question and then answer the question and nothing else. Do you understand that?"

The colonel remained silent.

"Colonel Brain, did you hear me?"

The colonel nodded violently and said nothing.

"Colonel Brain!" thundered the judge.

"Your Lordship told me only to answer the question and nothing else—or was that the question, my Lord? I really am finding this most terribly difficult."

"Not more than I am," said the judge, suddenly relaxing.

"Now, look, Colonel Brain," he went on in a kindly voice, "I realize that you may not have given evidence before and——"

"But I have, my Lord, I was telling your Lordship that——"

"Colonel Brain," went on the judge, still gently, "would you like to sit down while you give your evidence?"

"No, thank you, my Lord. I'm trying to stand to attention."

"So that's why you look so uncomfortable? It's quite unnecessary. Stand at ease or whatever the word is, Colonel."

"Thank you, my Lord. Your Lordship is most considerate. I'm afraid I can't get my feet the regulation distance apart, but as your Lordship can't see them, I hope——"

"Never mind about the feet, Colonel. Tell me about the man who came to see you yesterday. Who was he?"

"A Mr. Low, my Lord."

"Mr. Low? D'you mean the witness for the prosecution?"

"I believe he is, my Lord."

"And what did he say?"

"He told me that Mr. Morland hadn't said, 'I'll give you the opportunity'. But, of course, he was wrong, my Lord, as I told him. He had said it."

"That will do for the moment, thank you, Colonel Brain. Let Mr. Low come forward."

Mr. Low's evidence had already been given and he was accordingly in court. The previous day he had spent a fruitless half-hour with the colonel trying to disindoctrinate him but without success.

"Did you hear what Colonel Brain said?" the judge asked him.

"Yes, my Lord."

"Was it true?"

"Well," conceded Mr. Low, "I have been trying to persuade the colonel to be accurate in his evidence."

"Do you realize that interfering with a witness is a very serious matter?"

"I suppose it is, my Lord."

"And that's what you've been doing?"

Mr. Low said nothing in reply. There really was nothing to say.

"Well—have you anything to say about the matter? It is a

114

very serious contempt of court, and, unless you have some very good explanation—if, indeed, there can be one—I propose to treat it accordingly and to send you to prison."

"Well, my Lord, I was only trying to get him to state the facts—and not some garbled version of the facts which he'd got into his head somehow."

"You were trying to persuade him to change his evidence."

"His evidence was incorrect, my Lord."

"So you say, and you were trying to persuade him to change it."

"I suppose I was, my Lord."

"Very well then. It is difficult to conceive a clearer case of contempt of court. You will go to prison."

"For how long, my Lord?"

"Until you have purged your contempt."

"How can I do that, my Lord?"

"First by staying in prison."

"For how long, my Lord?"

"I shall consider that in due course. Secondly, by tendering such an apology to the Court as shows that you appreciate your offence and will never repeat it. No—it's no use offering apologies now. I will consider any regrets you have to offer after you have been lodged in prison for what I consider a sufficient period to teach you and any one else who may be similarly minded that witnesses must not be interfered with. And now, I think I shall rise. I think, perhaps, we've all had enough for the day."

Unpleasant as his imprisonment was to Mr. Low, his displeasure was nothing to the consternation it caused Jill, and only to a slightly less extent Alec. Although from time to time they had mistrusted him, he had always seemed so sure of himself and so confident that they had begun to believe in him completely. As long as he was in command behind the scenes, all would be well. And now he was in prison. Jill became almost desperate.

CHAPTER XII

ELIZABETH

ELIZABETH was at home knitting when Jill came to her. She was in tears.

"He's—he's gone to prison," she said eventually. Elizabeth did her best to comfort her and then suddenly realized that what Jill had said didn't make sense. Alec could only be found guilty or not guilty of murder. There was no possibility of a verdict of manslaughter in his case. The judge could only pass sentence of death if he were convicted and discharge him if he were acquitted.

"I don't understand," said Elizabeth. "I'd no idea the trial could be over so soon anyway."

"It isn't," said Jill, sobbing.

"Well—of course, he has to stay in prison. You can't have bail in a murder case. You've known that for a long time. What is it that's troubling you?"

"I'm not talking of Alec," said Jill.

"Not talking of Alec—then who's gone to prison?"

"Your husband."

"What did you say?"

"Your husband."

"But why?"

"Contempt of court."

"What did he do?"

"Apparently he tried to make Colonel Brain alter his evidence."

"Tell the truth, you mean."

"The judge didn't like it."

"No, of course, he wouldn't. Well, well, well," said Elizabeth, "after all these years." She could not help reflecting how ironical it was that her husband, who had risked imprisonment for serious crimes on numerous occasions but had never even been charged with one of them, had now been sent to prison for trying to persuade a witness to state what happened instead of what had not happened.

"Well," she said, after a moment or two's thought, "there's no time to be lost. We've a lot to do. You must pull yourself together. Get me a car quickly. Ring up a hire service. I want one with good springs and a careful driver. I don't want any accidents. And I'll want someone who'll drive me all night if necessary."

An hour later Elizabeth was on her way to Cunningham Gaol. Although it was late, she managed to obtain permission to see her husband.

"You are a blithering idiot," she said.

"I know—I know, but that doesn't help. You'll have to take on where I left off."

"That's why I'm here."

"Good for you. Now, look, I've an idea. It's a bit of a risk, but we've got to do something. I should go and see your father first and see if it's all right."

"I'm not going to tell him all about it."

"No, of course not, but find out if it's fairly safe. We don't want you in Holloway. Fancy having to call him Holloway Low. Sounds awful. Anyway, you'll have to tell your father I'm here. P'raps he can get me out. After all, I got him out once."

Sir Edwin Prout, Elizabeth's father, lived in a comfortable little cottage in the country. As a result of a stroke which he suffered while saving a child from a motorist and a series of accidents, he had been charged with murder and eventually, not only acquitted, but proved innocent, largely owing to Mr. Low's ingenuity. After his acquittal, he retired from the Bench and went to live in the country, where he was looked after by a housekeeper. He never knew the truth about his son-in-law's criminal past and thought him an amusing and intelligent person and an excellent husband for Elizabeth. He looked forward to their visits, but he was surprised at Elizabeth's sudden unannounced arrival.

"Why, Lizzie," he said, "how nice. But where's Ambrose? And why didn't you write or wire?"

"Ambrose is in prison."

117

"Nonsense."

"He is really, Father. It's all a silly mistake, but the judge at Cunningham Assizes thinks he was trying to interfere with a witness."

"But if he wasn't, why did he commit him?"

"He thought he was."

"But that's nonsense. Judges don't send people to prison like that."

"They do sometimes, Father—very, very occasionally, of course. But don't let's worry about Ambrose. There are some questions I want to ask you."

"But I do worry about him. I'm sure he's not the sort of chap to do anything really wrong. There might be a mis-understanding. Have you got solicitors acting for him? And counsel? He must swear an affidavit explaining everything —you know what I mean. 'I didn't do it, really I didn't, but if I did (which I didn't), I'm terribly sorry.'"

"Father," said Eliazbeth, disregarding his last remark, "is it contempt of court to talk to a witness?"

"Depends on the circumstances. First of all, do you know he's a witness? If you don't, of course you can talk to him. Otherwise a witness couldn't live while a trial was on. Even if you do know he's a witness, you can talk to him."

"About the case?"

"It depends what you say. Witnesses must talk about cases in which they're giving evidence to dozens of people."

"What mustn't you say?"

"Well—you mustn't try to interfere with the due course of justice. You mustn't, for example, try to persuade a witness to say something which isn't true or to forget something or not to attend on his subpœna."

"But if you just went and chatted to a witness, there'd be no harm in that?"

"Of course not."

"Even if someone had been sent to prison for contempt for trying to interfere with that very witness?"

"So that's what it was. Someone else had been interfering and poor Ambrose was suspected because of that. I am sorry. Now, let me see——"

"Would it be contempt to go and see a witness if someone else had been committed for trying to influence his evidence, Father?"

"Depends what you said to him. If you didn't discuss the case, of course it wouldn't be contempt. Even if you did, it wouldn't necessarily be contempt. But of course, if one man's been committed for contempt in relation to that witness, it would obviously be dangerous to go and discuss the case with him. Your object might be misconstrued—and your words."

"But provided you didn't in fact discuss that case, it wouldn't be a contempt?"

"No, of course not. Why—where are you off to?"

For Elizabeth had started to give her father what he knew from experience was a good-bye kiss.

"Must go and see about Ambrose, Father. We'll soon have him out. Sorry to be in such a rush."

And she was gone.

Fortunately for Elizabeth, Colonel Brain was in the meantime having rather a late session with Bobbie.

"Now, my boy," said the colonel, "if I'm not quite as bright as usual, you must forgive me. I've had rather a trying time in Court. They're good chaps, these judges, but very difficult to understand. And they don't seem to understand me very well. I was a bit worried at first when they started threatening to send me to prison, but I suppose it's all just part of the game, and they don't really mean it. Like the expressions we had in the Army, now I come to think of it. There's not much ease about standing at ease—not in a decent regiment, anyway. But you don't want to hear about my troubles, my boy. We must get down to this letter."

"You're terribly kind, Colonel. I do hope it's not too much of a bore."

"Not at all, my dear boy. Takes my mind off judges and prison and all that. Now, where had we got to?"

"We'd decided on 'Dear Alison' to begin with."

"Is that all? Never mind. One has to start somewhere."

"We hadn't made up our minds whether to try shock tactics or not."

"That's right, of course, my boy. Well, which is it to be? After all, you're going to marry the girl, not I. So you have the

119

right to decide. Even if I disagreed, I should give in. You're in command. I'm your staff officer. That's what it is. I'm the adjutant and you're the C.O. I do all the work and you take the kicks. Now, I would suggest, sir, if I may, that we start like this. From Robert Archer to Alison Hepworth. Subject: Marriage."

"I thought we were starting with 'Dear Alison', Colonel."

"Of course we were, my boy. I got carried away with the idea of writing a military letter. No 'dear' or 'yours sincerely' about that. Just 'from', 'to', and the subject. But you're right, of course. Too stiff for a proposal, so 'Dear Alison' it is. And, now, where do we go from there? Bit of a teaser, isn't it, my boy? I must think."

After a few moments' thought, the colonel said: "You're not in favour of poetry, I suppose. 'Hail to thee, blithe spirit', or something of that sort?"

"I'm not sure how she'd take it, Colonel. Her feet are very firmly on the ground. Though, of course, she's read a terrible lot."

"Well, my boy, how about some flattery first? Never does any harm with a woman. They'll take almost anything. So I've found. What about this? 'Your feet—firm on the ground, though they be—are very small.' Humph! You don't think much of it? Well, quite candidly, my boy, neither do I. But one has to try, or one wouldn't get anywhere. And it was better than 'Your feet, firm on the ground though they be, are very large'. I don't believe in rudeness. Politeness costs nothing. If a chap barges into me in the street, I always apologize. Much the best way—even if it's my own fault. Makes him think it's his. Now, we must really get on."

At that moment the bell rang. It was Elizabeth.

"I'm so sorry, my dear chap. Forgive me."

He left Bobbie and opened the front door. He had seen Elizabeth before, but had never met her. She introduced herself and apologized for calling so late.

"Not at all, my dear lady, not at all. I'm so very sorry about your husband. I do hope he's as comfortable as possible."

"That's most kind of you. I wonder if I could see you alone for a few minutes."

"Most certainly. I'm sorry, my boy," and he turned to Bobbie. "I'm afraid we'll have to break off again. But we're getting on, you know. Soon be finished now. Good night, my boy."

Bobbie left, and the colonel immediately looked expectantly at Elizabeth.

"You've come to talk about the case, I suppose?" he said.

"Good gracious, no," said Elizabeth. "Anything but. I don't want to go to prison too."

"Of course," said the colonel. "How silly of me. We won't mention it. Or I'll be going to prison as well. Pretty dreadful the way these judges send us off to gaol. Everyone except the chap in the dock. Still, I suppose that's what they're there for. No use being a judge unless you pop 'em inside from time to time."

Elizabeth laughed. "You're quite a wit, Colonel," she said.

"You don't say," said the colonel, "you don't say. As a matter of fact, now you come to mention it, they used to laugh a bit in the mess after I'd said something. It must have been that, I suppose. I didn't realize it at the time."

"One often doesn't, Colonel. It's extraordinary how one doesn't appreciate what other people are driving at sometimes until long afterwards."

"Very true, my dear lady, very true."

"Sometimes a person will say something to you and you'll think he's quite serious. Then, after he's left, you realize it was only a joke."

"D'you think the judge was serious when he sent your husband to prison? P'raps that was only a joke."

"No, I'm afraid that was serious. But it's different in Court. You like a good joke, I expect, Colonel?"

"No one more, dear lady."

"The funniest things are sometimes said most seriously, don't you think? Dry humour's the most effective. If a man slips on a banana skin, some people laugh, but it isn't really funny."

"Not funny at all, dear lady. Very painful too. And dangerous. I knew a man who broke a bone that way. Nothing amusing about that. In hospital for weeks. I used to go and see him.

121

He was a cheerful chap, though. D'you know what he said when I first went to see him?"

"No," said Elizabeth, "I don't think I do."

"No—you wouldn't, would you? Well—he'd broken a bone by slipping on the pavement and sitting down too hard, if I may mention such a thing. And what d'you think he said when I first went to see him? 'Hullo, Beefie, old man,' he said. 'What d'you think I'm here for? For saving life at sea,' he said. 'For saving life at sea.' I laughed till I ached—until I suddenly realized I couldn't see the point. What d'you think he meant—for saving life at sea? He fell down in Paddington. No sea there. P'raps he meant the Canal. But it's not tidal, you know. Is that what you'd call dry humour?"

"Not very," said Elizabeth.

"Still, it was good to see him so cheerful. He had a pretty nurse too. That helped, I suppose. He offered to marry her in the end."

"That wasn't a joke, I suppose?"

"No joke at all, dear lady. I was the best man. He changed his mind at the last moment and asked me to take his place. D'you know, I'd almost done it when I realized I couldn't. No banns and all that. That was a narrow squeak and no mistake. I don't know what my housekeeper would have said. I'd have had to have brought the girl home. Couldn't very well have left her in the porch. However, she did very well in the end. Sued my friend for breach and bought some pictures with the damages. The artist was thrown in with the pictures. So she got a husband after all, at least that's how it was told to me."

"I think that's most amusing," said Elizabeth. "It's curious what a lot of amusement there is in life. And as I said before, so many things which seem serious at the time are meant to be jokes."

"You think so?"

"I don't just think so. It is so. A man comes up to you with a very straight face and says: 'I've cut my wife's throat.' He doesn't mean it. Just his idea of a joke. Not a good one, I agree."

"Might I ask who he was, dear lady? In case I meet him. I might take him seriously."

"How right you are, Colonel. That is the danger. As a

matter of fact, that wasn't a real example, but you do get plenty of them, you know. 'What have you been doing?' you ask. 'Shooting my gamekeeper, as a matter of fact.' "

"Did he really? An accident, I suppose. They will happen, of course. I know a brigadier who peppered his batman once."

"No, it wasn't an accident, Colonel. It was just a joke. He thought it would be funny to say it. That must have happened to you sometimes, you know."

"You think so?"

"I'm sure of it. When some big event has just taken place—a murder or something—people will often say—just in fun, of course—that they've done it. It's just a silly kind of joke."

Elizabeth stopped speaking for a moment, and then said rather slowly:

"D'you know, Colonel, if you don't mind my saying so, I believe you're inclined to take people too seriously. If you cast your mind back—can't you think of occasions when you've understood people too literally?"

"Well, you know, my dear lady, my memory isn't as good as it was. So I can't cast the old mind back as far as I'd like, but perhaps you're right."

"I'm sure I am, Colonel. Of course—it doesn't matter in the normal way, but occasionally it might get people into trouble. For instance—supposing you asked me where I got this umbrella from and I said: 'As a matter of fact, I pinched it from the Stores' and you went and reported me and I couldn't produce a receipt—look how awkward it would be for me. Don't you see?"

The colonel looked doubtfully at the umbrella and then at Elizabeth. "Well, you can rely on me, dear lady," he said at last. "I won't tell a soul. But, if it isn't rude of me—why did you do it? Oh—I suppose it's your husband in gaol and all that. But"— and he shook his head gravely— "take the advice of an older man, dear lady—honesty's the best policy. The other thing doesn't pay."

"Have you tried the other thing, Colonel, then?"

"Certainly not, dear lady. What a thought! Bang would go the old pension. Not worth it, don't you see?"

"I was only joking, Colonel."

"I'm glad to hear it, dear lady. You had me worried for a moment. Don't you think p'raps you'd better take the umbrella back?"

"I was only joking about that too, Colonel. I've had it for years. Don't you see, that's what I mean about your taking things too seriously."

"'Pon my soul, dear lady, I believe you're right. But how am I to know when a thing's serious or not?"

"Well, Colonel—in the first place, people don't confess to serious crimes to strangers or acquaintances. It doesn't make sense, does it?"

Elizabeth spent another hour working on the colonel, but she never once mentioned the case of Alec Morland. Before she left she said: "Colonel, I think perhaps it would be as well if you didn't mention this conversation to anyone. People might think I'd talked to you about the case."

"Not a word, dear lady. I might end up in prison too. Silly that one can't have an ordinary conversation without being frightened of going to gaol. But there it is, the law's an ass, dear lady, but it can kick like one too sometimes."

"And bray too sometimes, Colonel."

"How right you are—but I won't say you said it or you'd certainly be for it. Fancy telling his Lordship that the law brayed. He'd have you in irons—or whatever they put ladies in these days. I can hear him saying it. 'Put her in plastic, gaoler', he'd say. 'And as for you, sir', and then he'd turn on me, 'how dare you! I'll make an example of you. You'll go to prison for, let me see!—and then he'd count on his fingers—'one, two, three, four, five'—then he'd go to the other hand—lucky he can't reach his feet, I say—but I'm keeping you, dear lady. So very pleased to have seen you. Mum's the word, to coin a phrase."

Elizabeth left the colonel. She was a little exhausted by her efforts, but she had enough strength left to complete the remainder of the operation, which was to send an anonymous letter to Duffield. At the time she was posting it, he was in bed talking to his wife.

"But it sounds as though it's going really well," said Laura. "I can't think why you're so depressed."

"It is going well, in a way—except for that oaf of a colonel. If only I could smash him, it would probably be all right, but it doesn't look as though I can."

"I dare say—but does he matter so much? Surely no one's going to take too much notice of what he says?"

"Well—yes and no. You see—it's Alec I'm worrying about. With Colonel Brain's evidence I can't possibly submit that there's no case to answer. And once Alec goes into the box I think we'll be sunk."

"Why?"

"He's such a rotten liar."

"What d'you mean? Has he told you he's done it? I thought you couldn't defend him if he had."

"No, of course he hasn't. But if he's no better in the witness box than he is when I cross-examined him at the prison, he's almost bound to go down."

It is a normal rule that counsel does not personally see the witnesses he is going to call or ask them any questions directly, with the exception of his own client. But he is entitled to see his own client as much as he likes and to question him about the case as much as he likes. The result ordinarily is that his own client has already had a dress rehearsal for the cross-examination which is likely to be administered by the opposing side in Court. This is, of course, a tremendous advantage, particularly if the client's counsel is able.

"They're bound to ask you about the letter of the fifteenth January," he'll say. "What's your answer to that?" The client will give some explanation. "But I don't follow," says counsel, "if that's the case, the interview must have been before the letter."

"Oh, yes," says the client, "I may have made a mistake. Let me think. Ah—yes. I've got it now. My explanation of the letter is this." And he proceeds to give a somewhat different explanation. Had this dialogue taken place in Court and had the cross-examination been by opposing counsel, the client might never have recovered from the awkward position in which he found himself. As it is, it was all done in his own counsel's chambers and the mistake will not be made. A very useful dress rehearsal indeed. But it can only take place in the normal

125

way with the client himself. With the other witnesses a more cumbersome process has to be adopted. Counsel will write in his advice on evidence something like this:

"Mr. Jones will no doubt be asked in cross-examination what his answer is to the letter of the 15th January. I should like to know what it is. If he says so-and-so, how does he explain such-and-such, and if he says such-and-such, how does he explain so-and-so?"

Given a really efficient solicitor or solicitor's managing clerk, a satisfactory dress rehearsal will take place in the solicitor's office. But the effectiveness of the rehearsal will depend upon the ability and thoroughness of the solicitor and his clerk. Possibly the witness's answers will be reported to counsel and he will write or suggest further questions to be asked of him. In other words, the same process will take place, but, as far as counsel is concerned, it will normally be by remote control in the case of all witnesses except the client and expert witnesses. It is easy to criticize this process and to ask why counsel should be allowed to rehearse the person who is possibly his most important witness—the client, if it is not considered desirable that he should rehearse the others. Why is it not desirable? it will be asked. Because rehearsing is too near to coaching. Well then, why should the client himself be allowed to be coached? The answer to this very reasonable question is really that if a man is not to be allowed to see his own advocate, he cannot have the faith in the proper presentation of his case, criminal or civil, which he ought to have. If the client, then, is to be allowed to see his counsel—and it is difficult to say that this should not be permitted—it is impossible to restrict the questions which counsel may ask him. It must be assumed that counsel will act properly and in good faith and, within those limits, it must be left to counsel to say to his client and ask him what he thinks fit. Of course, in criminal cases a greater latitude may perhaps be allowed to an advocate than in civil matters, it being so vital that everything should be done to see that no innocent man is convicted and that every accused has his case presented as well as possible.

Accordingly, in Morland's case Duffield had cross-examined him very thoroughly indeed in the room in the prison in which he interviewed him. He was really appalled at the result. His explanations of all his movements were not only sometimes lame in themselves, but were given so lamely that it was extremely difficult to believe in them. The trouble, of course, was that, as Duffield had said, Alec was not a good liar. He was not normally a liar at all. He was naturally desperately anxious to be acquitted, but the lies he would have to tell not only stuck in his throat but made fairly obvious swellings which Duffield was afraid the jury would not be able to help observing. Even Alec himself had said during the interview: "This is hopeless. I can see you don't believe me."

"It doesn't matter whether I believe you or not. It's the jury that counts."

"Well—if you don't believe me, are they likely to? Well—are they? All right, don't bother to answer. I can see what you think. For heaven's sake, don't tell Jill. I've told her it'll be all right. Have I got a chance at all—d'you think?"

"Everyone has a chance."

"But you think I'll go down, don't you? Be frank. I'd much prefer to know. You do, don't you?"

"Well—old boy—I'm bound to say your evidence isn't terribly convincing."

"I'll try and do better."

"If you are telling the truth—if only you could sound as if you were."

"I'll do my best, old boy. I'm afraid I'm a bit of a menace to you."

"Don't be absurd. But frankly it is your evidence I'm worried about. The case against you isn't too bad, but, as things are, you'll have to go into the witness box—and——"

"You don't fancy my chances when I do."

"One just can't tell. The jury will want to help you—but, well, if you don't do better than you did this afternoon, they'll have the devil of a difficulty."

Although Duffield did not discuss with his wife his actual conversation with Alec, he felt bound to warn her of what he feared.

"Perhaps he'll do better than you expect," said Laura.

"He can't do worse. The chap's too honest, that's the trouble. D'you know, I believe for two pins he'd say he'd done it. If only I could get the jury to stop the case before he gets into the box. I thought I should at one time, but this idiot of a colonel sticks to his story. I wish I'd taken that fellow Low's advice."

"What advice?"

"He told me to treat him gently at the Magistrates' Court. How he knew, heaven alone know. But, by going for him in that court, I've made him surer than ever. It was a bad error of judgment on my part."

"You couldn't help it. How could you tell what Low was getting at?"

"I couldn't, but that doesn't make it any better. If Alec's hanged, it may well be due to my cross-examination of Colonel Brain at the Magistrates' Court."

"It sounds awful. If Alec's hanged. D'you really think he will be?"

"Nothing's certain, but unless a miracle happens, he'll have to go into the box—and then, unless there's another miracle, he'll go down. And with the present Home Secretary, there's a good chance he won't reprieve him after the fuss there's been over that other case. Well, I must go to sleep, or I won't be fit to cross-examine the colonel or anything. Good night, my darling."

When Duffield got up next morning there was an anonymous letter for him. It gave him a few simple words of advice. This time he decided to take them.

CHAPTER XIII

THE NATURE OF A JOKE

ELIZABETH had stayed at Cunningham for the night. She got up early next morning and waited near the court in her hired car until she saw Colonel Brain. She went straight up to him..

"Ah—good morning, dear lady."

"Good morning, Colonel."

"I'm afraid I've a terrible confession to make, Colonel."

"A confession, dear lady? I shall love to hear it. Years since I heard one. I'm always having to make them, as a matter of fact. To my housekeeper, you know. Explaining lateness and all that."

"I'm terribly sorry, Colonel."

"Please don't be too upset, dear lady. Perhaps it isn't as bad as you think."

"You'll be terribly angry, I'm afraid."

"Never," protested the colonel.

"But you will be. You won't be able to help it."

"I'm sure I shall. The old self-control is still working. And, anyway, I can't think what you can have done to upset me. I enjoyed our little chat last night. Come, come," he went on, as Elizabeth seemed to hesitate, "it can't be as bad as all that."

"It is, I'm afraid," said Elizabeth, "you'll be furious."

"Well, I'm not so far. Did you leave something behind, is that it?"

"Oh—no—far worse."

"Dear me. It's not another umbrella? You haven't pinched one of my old umbrellas? You're very welcome to them all. They don't work. That I expect you know by now."

"Well—I know they don't work now—though I didn't take one, as a matter of fact."

"Then how do you know they don't work? Did you try them when you were there?"

"No, Colonel."

"This has me baffled, absolutely baffled, worse than some of the exams I failed. How d'you know they don't work?"

"Because nothing works at your house at the moment, Colonel."

"Well, my dear lady, I'm not angry, but it's a bit hard to put it that way. I do do the odd bit of gardening. But I suppose I could put a bit more into it. But my housekeeper—she works like anything. No—I must take issue with you there, dear lady. One of us works at home, anyway."

"I wasn't speaking of people, Colonel."

"Oh—clocks, you mean. Well—the one in the hall, I grant you, that doesn't go much. Every now and then it starts off. But the one in the kitchen's an alarm clock. That goes all right —woke me this morning, as a matter of fact."

"It doesn't go any more, Colonel."

"Doesn't go any more? But how d'you know, dear lady? It was going when I left home. At least, I thought it was. May have wanted winding, of course. Not like me to forget that. Always wind the clocks last thing. Except the one in the hall. That's once a week, when it's going. But I grant you that's more of an ornament than anything."

"Colonel—you will be terribly cross when I tell you. But please try to understand. Nothing works in your house now. Hadn't I better tell you why?"

"Come to think of it, dear lady, perhaps you had. Why, then?"

"Because I'm afraid I burned the whole house down just after you left this morning."

"Burned the house down, dear lady? But, really—that's too bad. That's terrible—but what about my housekeeper?"

"Oh—she's all right—she escaped."

"Good gracious me—but why—why—what made you do such a thing?"

"I'm afraid I just felt like burning down a house. So I burned yours."

"But it's a terrible thing to do. It's a police matter. You'll go to prison. What on earth possessed you? 'Pon my word, I thought you rather liked me. And now to go and burn my house down. Really—it can't be true. I can't believe it. Tell me it isn't true. Tell me I'm dreaming."

"You're not dreaming, Colonel, but it isn't true."

"Thank goodness. I was really worried. But why did you say it?"

"Don't you remember our conversation of last night, Colonel? It was just a joke. And you took it seriously again."

"By jove, you're right. By jove, you are. P'raps I do take things too seriously. Never thought of it like that before."

" Just imagine, Colonel, who on earth would confess to burning someone else's house down? Now you come to think of it, it could only have been a joke, Colonel. It couldn't have been anything else. Calmly standing in the High Street and saying I'd burned your house down. Might just as well say I'd killed your housekeeper. Could only be a joke, couldn't it?"

"Of course, dear lady. And a very good joke too. Haven't laughed so much for years. But, by jove, that's funny. I haven't started laughing at all—and I said I hadn't laughed so much for years." The colonel laughed heartily.

"I thought it might be nice to start the day with a joke, Colonel."

"That's very civil of you, dear lady. I'll try to think one up for you."

"Don't worry now, Colonel—but you really mustn't take people so seriously. They often say the most terrible things in fun."

"I won't forget. You won't catch me again. Jolly good. A joke, that's what it was. Must remember to tell my housekeeper."

"That's right, Colonel—a joke—and there are lots more about if you look for them."

"Lots of what, dear lady?"

"Jokes, Colonel, jokes, jokes, jokes." And Elizabeth left the colonel and went back to her car. As she got into the car, she said: "Now, Miss Low, there's nothing to laugh about yet. No —thank you, driver. I was just murmuring to myself."

While Elizabeth was putting the finishing touches to the colonel, her husband was talking to the Governor of Cunningham prison.

"I don't like it here, sir," said Mr. Low.

"I dare say you don't," said the Governor. "A lot of people share your opinion."

"I want to get out."

"There again, you'll find a lot of people think the same."

"I want to make an application to be released. May I see a solicitor?"

"Yes, we can arrange that. Whom d'you want to see?"

"I'm not sure. Any competent solicitor. And counsel, too, perhaps."

"Well, it's not my business to advise you on the choice of

131

solicitors, but there is quite a good firm here called Milton and Regis. They do a lot of the work in Cunningham."

"Could I see them at once, sir?"

"I can't promise that, but I'll get someone to give them a ring and see if they can send a representative. But they're pretty busy people. You may have to wait a bit. But I'll tell them it's urgent. It is, I suppose?"

"The liberty of the subject, sir. That should take precedence of goods sold and delivered."

"Very well. I'll see what can be done."

Messrs. Milton and Regis were indeed an extremely busy firm of country solicitors and did more work than any other firm in the neighbourhood. Nevertheless, when Mr. Regis heard the nature of the inquiry, he immediately stopped investigating the title to a farm which a client of his was buying, sent for his car, and drove to the prison. This would be far more interesting, he said to himself, and give him more to say at the golf club. He had not been pleased that his firm was not concerned in the trial at all. They usually acted on one side or another in all important cases, and it was annoying that his old friend and rival, Tom Malling, had been instructed for the defence. Now, almost at the last moment, he was in the case too. Tom wouldn't have it all his own way at the nineteenth hole. William Regis was a stout, good-natured man, full of fun if not of humour. He was only moderately intelligent and capable of saying with emphasis the exact opposite of what he had been saying the minute before. He said it with sincerity, too, because as often as not he was unaware that he had changed his mind or that someone else had changed it for him.

Mr. Low was delighted to see him arrive so soon after his conversation with the Governor.

"Dear, dear, dear," said Mr. Regis, after he had been introduced to Mr. Low. "This is a pretty pass. Not too comfortable here, I'm afraid. You can have food sent in though, if you want. I once had a client who lived here almost entirely on oysters. In the season, of course."

"How did he manage when it was over?"

"He applied for his release."

"I see. He was lucky."

"He wasn't. He didn't get it. That was the joke," and Mr. Regis laughed boisterously. "He came out in the end, though. Let me see, was it six months or a year he did? I'm not sure. That's the trouble with contempt. So indefinite. Theoretically it can go on for ever. But don't let me get you down. Only my fun, you know. Now, what is it I can do for you?"

"I want to apply to get out."

"You've only just come in."

"That's why. I don't like it."

"Don't like it, eh? Well—you won't mind my saying I'm glad they're not too comfortable. Enough burglaries as it is. But I mustn't waste time. I read about your committal, of course. But I can't see old Pantin letting you out yet, after what he said."

"I know it may be difficult. But I thought perhaps if I explained."

"Explained what?"

"How it all happened. I don't think I did myself justice at the time. I wasn't ready for it."

"Well—we can try, but I don't suppose it'll be any good. You'll probably be chucking your money away. But if you don't mind that."

"I'll take a chance on it."

"Well—I'll get hold of counsel. There are several good chaps here for the Assizes. I'll see if Kingsdown can do it—the son of the late judge, you know. He'll be as good as any. I'll run down and see if I can get hold of him now. He's got an accident case for us in the other court, but I don't suppose it'll be on till this afternoon. See you again shortly, I hope."

At the Assize Court, Pomeroy was chatting to Duffield just before they went into court.

"I'd like to see your chap get away with it," he said.

"So would he," said Duffield.

"It should be over today, I suppose. Depends how many witnesses you're calling."

"I'm not sure."

"You're going to open the case then?"

"That's the one certain thing. I'm going to open the case."

"You don't want the last word then?"

"I do, indeed."

"Don't follow, old boy."

In criminal cases counsel for the defence has the right to make his final speech to the jury after the prosecution, if he calls no witnesses other than the prisoner or witnesses as to character only, but, in that case, he is not entitled to address the jury before calling his evidence. Pomeroy could not, therefore, understand how Duffield could say that he intended to open the case—which must imply that he was going to call witnesses and therefore entitle counsel for the Crown to make his final address to the jury after counsel for the defence, and, at the same time, say that he wanted the last word.

"I hope you will," said Duffield. "And now for Colonel Brain."

They walked into court and, as soon as the judge and jury were in their places, the colonel went back into the witness box.

"You are still on oath, Colonel," said the judge. "Has anyone spoken to you about the case since yesterday?"

"No one, my Lord. I could swear to that, if necessary."

"You have sworn to it, Colonel."

"My memory isn't as good as it was, my Lord. I thought that was yesterday."

"I have just told you that you are still on oath."

"I thought that was a figure of speech, my Lord. I often say that kind of thing myself. The other day, for instance, I said to my housekeeper, 'I would take an oath on that', I said—it was something about being late—I forget the details—but I don't suppose your Lordship would want them. Indeed, I didn't know I was going to be asked about them, as a matter of fact. If your Lordship would forgive me, I would go and fetch my housekeeper and no doubt she'd be able to help me. I shan't be a moment, my Lord."

And the colonel started to leave the witness box.

"Colonel Brain," said the judge, quite gently, "don't go away, please."

"If your Lordship prefers me to stay——"

"I do."

"Well, of course, my Lord."

"Thank you."

Colonel Brain bowed to the judge and waited.

"Now, where were we?" said the judge, after a moment. "I've forgotten now."

"Ah, my Lord," began the colonel.

"No—don't interrupt, please, Colonel. Oh—yes—I was reminding you that you took an oath yesterday to tell the truth, the whole truth, and nothing but the truth."

"Nothing but the truth," said the colonel solemnly. "I hope I haven't made a mistake anywhere."

"I hope not, too, Colonel."

"That's very good of your Lordship."

"And I asked you if you'd discussed the case with anyone since yesterday, and you said you could swear you hadn't."

"That's right, my Lord. Shall I take the oath?"

"I had just reminded you, Colonel, that you took the oath yesterday."

"Oh yes, my Lord. But not today."

"The oath continues, Colonel. It is unnecessary to take it again."

"But how long for, my Lord?" asked the colonel, a little anxiously. "I mean, suppose I'm a bit late, when I get home— it's going to be rather awkward if I can't stretch a point every now and then."

"It only continues during your evidence at this trial."

"That's a relief, my Lord. Perhaps I'd better stay here till it's over."

"Now, don't let's waste any more time, Colonel. You are now on oath, Colonel. Do you understand that?"

The colonel came to attention and then slightly raised his right hand and lowered it again quickly.

"I'm sorry, my Lord."

"Sorry?"

"My Lord, I'm afraid I nearly saluted. Forgot I hadn't my cap on."

"But you're not in uniform either, Colonel."

"Gracious," said the colonel. "Nor I am. It was the authority in your Lordship's voice which did it."

The judge sighed. "Do you realize you are on oath, Colonel?" he said, after a moment's pause.

"Of course, if your Lordship says so, but I haven't taken it to-day, my Lord."

"Let the witness be sworn again," said the judge. "I've had enough of this nonsense. I can't think you're as simple-minded as all that, Colonel, and I warn you that, if you're trying to be funny, you'll go to prison for a very long time."

"There it is again," said the colonel to himself. "Oh, dear, I'm sure I shall end up there."

After the colonel had taken the oath, the judge asked him again: "Have you spoken about the case to anyone since yesterday?"

"No, my Lord, I can swear to that."

"You *are* on oath, Colonel."

"I know, my Lord, that's why I said I could swear to it."

"Will you continue your cross-examination, please, Mr. Duffield."

"Colonel Brain," said Duffield, "this conversation you had with the prisoner—d'you think it can have been in the nature of a joke?"

To Elizabeth, listening in the gallery, it seemed an age before the colonel answered the question. But at last he did so.

"In the nature of a joke, did you say, sir?"

CHAPTER XIV

SPEECH FOR THE DEFENCE

The case for the prosecution ended not long before the luncheon adjournment, but there was time for Duffield to begin his speech.

"Members of the jury," he said, "you have been listening for some time—and no doubt with the greatest care—to a case which may well be unexampled in the history of the criminal courts. A man is charged with the crime of saving life—but the name given to that crime in this Court is murder. Now, let me say this at once. My learned friend, with his usual fairness, has pointed out to you that the object of this crime—for unquestionably the killing of Gilbert Essex, criminal though he was and a bestial criminal at that, was a crime—the object of this crime is irrelevant to a consideration of your verdict. He has said to you that the only question you have to consider is whether the prisoner killed Essex or not. May I—with my usual fairness—say that I certainly agree with him. However wellintentioned the object of the killing may have been, it has nothing to do with the case—unless, indeed, it could, in certain circumstances, be said to weigh against the prisoner. By that I mean this—if you think the prisoner had a motive for killing Essex—albeit, in one sense, an excellent motive—to save the lives of women whom the dead man would undoubtedly have killed if he, himself, had not been killed—then the prosecution will have shown—what they have no need to show, but which, of course, they may show if they can—a motive for this crime. I make them a present of that. There was a motive for the crime—a motive, I suppose, which could be present in the minds of all the adult population in this country who knew of the crimes of Gilbert Essex and of the inability of the police to check them. Some of you—indeed, possibly all of you—may have said to yourselves at one time or another: 'Something must be done to stop these murders. Why don't the police act ? It can't go on like this. I wish I could do something myself. I pray that I may read in the papers that he has been caught. No woman will be safe until he is.' Members of the jury, your prayers were answered. Gilbert Essex will kill no more."

"Mr. Duffield," interrupted the judge, "I am always loath to intervene when counsel is addressing the jury, but there is a limit, you know. You are not entitled to tempt the jury to acquit the accused just because good may have resulted from the crime."

"My Lord," said Duffield, "I was just about to say that. I was just about to say, members of the jury, that I am not asking you to acquit my client out of thankfulness or any similar motives. If you are satisfied that the prisoner killed Essex, that is an end of the matter, however thankful you may be, and you must convict him. I should not, in those circumstances, ask—indeed, as his Lordship has pointed out—I am not entitled to ask for any other verdict. If Alec Morland killed Gilbert Essex—though his motives were the best in the world—you must say that he is guilty—and he must die. It is not for you or me to consider the consequences of your verdict. You are not concerned with the penalty—with the end it may—or you may think, in view of recent events, it assuredly will—put to a useful life, a life spent in years not long past in the devoted service of his country. I am not entitled, members of the jury, to pray in aid that service—that long and, I repeat, devoted service—as a ground for your acquitting the prisoner—except to this extent—I am entitled to ask you to say that, as against a man of his sterling and proved good character, the prosecution has not—even at this stage—even before my client says a word in his own defence—the prosecution has not proved its case. In due course, members of the jury, I shall—if necessary—if necessary, call the prisoner and other evidence, but at every stage of this trial it is for the prosecution to prove its case. It is not for the accused to prove his innocence. So then, members of the jury, granting as I do, without the slightest qualification, that the only question you have to decide is whether this prisoner killed this murderer, I propose to examine with you, if you will bear with me, the evidence which the Crown has called to establish his guilt. And I am going to do so at this stage, members of the jury, because you have now heard the whole of the evidence upon which the Crown relies—and it is open to you, at any moment—now—if you are so minded—to say that, even without a word from the prisoner, you are not satisfied of his guilt and that this nightmare which he and his wife and friends and relatives have been enduring for so long should end —and should end now. And let me add just one word before I examine the evidence. Just as my learned friend—and, I hope, I myself have explained to you, not once but several times— that the result of a conviction is no concern of yours—so the result of your acquitting him is equally no concern. Though, in that connection, I cannot think that any one of you will believe that a verdict of Not Guilty in this case will result in people taking the law into their own hands. Even if you were afraid that the police might be as incompetent in other cases as they were in the case of Gilbert Essex, you must not allow that fact to influence your verdict by one iota. But I am sure you won't, members of the jury. I am sure that you will consider only what it is your duty to consider. And, at this stage, you may well care to examine in some detail the evidence for the prosecution. During the adjournment which will shortly follow, you may well think it worth while to see on what evidence it is that the Crown says that this accused is guilty of murder. I venture to suggest to you that, when you do examine that evidence, you will find that it is lamentably—well, perhaps lamentably is not at all the right word for me to use—splendidly is more appropriate for counsel for the defence to use—is not the evidence splendidly lacking in that degree of proof necessary for conviction on a criminal charge—even a much lesser one than murder? As my learned friend has told you—very fairly—suspicion is not enough. Proof is required—and what proof is there? I submit to you, members of the jury, that there is none. Someone may say or think—'But proof, in some cases, is difficult'. All right—so it is—but because it is difficult, that is no reason for dispensing with it. On the contrary. Now, what proof is there in this case? When you examine the evidence, I suggest to you that there is none at all—none at all. There are, if you like, grounds for suspicion now and then, but, in my submission, that is putting the case for the prosecution at the highest. Gilbert Essex was killed by being struck on the head, rendered unconscious or helpless, and being thrown over a cliff. Who saw him struck on the head? No one. Who heard him cry out? No one. But there was someone near, you know—the witness Rose Lee. She heard and saw nothing. She was running away, the prosecution will say. So she was. But the fact that she had good reason for not seeing or hearing anything doesn't prove the affirmative that it was my client who struck the blow. There was someone who might have identified my client as the man who killed Essex, but she didn't. But, members of the jury, she did hear someone speak. And here I agree with my learned friend, there can be little doubt but that the man she heard speak was the man who in fact did the killing. Well—did she recognize my client's voice as the voice she heard? As you know, she did not. It was not even a case of her saying she didn't know. When she heard my client's voice, she said—it is well within your recollection—she said that she did not think that was the voice. Well, members of the jury, what more do you want? You might have thought she was a witness for the defence. The prosecution have to prove it was my client's voice and the best they can do is to call someone who thinks it wasn't. There's proof for you, members of the jury! There's evidence to convict a man of murder! Would you convict a man of proved bad character on such evidence? Of course you wouldn't. Then, what about my client, whose character you know? But, of course, there was other evidence. It is no good my not being fair—that would only harm my client. If I leave out any of the evidence, you would notice it. And I don't intend to do so. I shall examine each piece of evidence. and I hope you will do so too. And—if it won't interfere with your digestions—I suggest you do so at lunch, members of the jury—because, quite frankly, members of the jury, I am inviting you here and now to stop this case—to stop the agony for my client and his wife and friends. But I don't ask you to do that out of hand—but only after thinking of every piece of evidence the prosecution have been able to bring."

Duffield then proceeded to go through all the evidence called against the prisoner, pointing out its insufficiency here, ridiculing it there, and reminding the jury that the cumulative effect of nothing added to nothing is still nothing, however many times you repeat the process.

"And now, members of the jury," he went on, "I come to the evidence of Colonel Brain, a witness who, I don't suggest for a moment, has come here to tell you anything which he does not believe to be the truth—when he can remember it. And what did his evidence come to after all? It is only a little while ago that it tumbled to the ground like a pack of cards. That conversation between him and the prisoner, that conversation which my learned friend opened to you as an admission of guilt—what did it turn out to be but just a joke? Indeed, by the time I had finished cross-examining the colonel, he professed himself as unable to understand that he'd said anything else from the start. 'I laughed like anything,' he said, 'so did the prisoner.' 'I thought it was the best joke I'd heard for years', he said. You remember, members of the jury. Well—members of the jury, can you conceive a guilty man admitting his guilt to a stranger? I suppose it's possible, if he were drunk—or if he were a person of a different character from that of my client. But can you conceive a man like my client seriously admitting his guilt to his part-time gardener? A silly jest, perhaps—but an admission of guilt. I suggest to you it doesn't bear thinking about."

"I think," interrupted the judge, "this will be a convenient moment to adjourn for lunch."

"If your Lordship pleases."

"My Lord," said a barrister, who had not so far taken any part in the proceedings, " would it be convenient to your Lordship to mention the case of Ambrose Low before your Lordship rises?"

"Certainly not, Mr. Kingsdown," said his Lordship, and rose.

CHAPTER XV

LUNCH FOR TWELVE

"WOULD you mind passing the horseradish sauce, please?" said the foreman of the jury to the neighbour on his left, a middle-aged, inoffensive little man. He was apparently shy and retiring and had hardly exchanged a word with any of his fellows during the three days of the trial. Nothing happened. "The horseradish sauce, please," the foreman repeated. Still nothing happened.

"I'm sorry to trouble you," said the foreman more loudly, "but might I have the horseradish sauce!"

As the inoffensive little man still did nothing and the foreman's voice could now be heard right down the table, the jurywoman on the left of the inoffensive looking man said to him: "Excuse me, but could you pass the horseradish sauce to your right?"

The inoffensive little man apparently came out of his dreams. "I'm so sorry," he said, turning to the jurywoman, "did you say something?" The foreman, seeing that his neighbour was now awake, repeated his request quite quietly. But his neighbour took no notice and continued to look expectantly at the jurywoman. As the foreman had said what he wanted, she said nothing.

"I'm so sorry," repeated the inoffensive little man, still looking at the jurywoman, "did you say something?"

A sudden and dreadful thought came into the foreman's mind. Speaking in a normal voice, he said: "You're not deaf, by any chance?" The juryman addressed took no notice. The foreman touched him on the shoulder and said to him loudly: "You're not deaf, by any chance?"

"Eh—what's that? Deaf—yes—I'm afraid I am rather."

There was complete silence in the room. Hands, with knives or forks in them, remained in the air, mouths remained closed or open. Movement and mastication were temporarily suspended. After a moment, the foreman said, fairly loudly, but in a voice which did not conceal his anxiety: "Have you heard anything that's happened in Court?"

"Oh—yes——" began the man, and the foreman and his fellow jurors started to relax—but all too soon. "A little," went on the inoffensive looking man. The anxiety returned. Everyone had the same thought. How could they tell the judge, after three days, that one of the jury had only heard a little of what had been going on? It did not require much imagination to visualize the judge's reaction. 'And,' thought the foreman, 'I'll be the one who has to tell him. It just can't be done.'

"For heaven's sake," he said aloud, "why didn't you say you couldn't hear?"

"I beg your pardon?" said the inoffensive looking man.

The foreman repeated the question loudly.

"I didn't like to," was the answer. "I'm a bit shy about it, I suppose."

"What about your oath?" said the man opposite.

"I beg your pardon?" said the inoffensive looking man.

"Your oath," the man almost shouted. "You swore to give a true verdict according to the evidence. How can you do that if you haven't heard it?"

"Well," said the inoffensive looking man, uncomfortably, "there's only one of me and I thought that, if you all thought alike, I couldn't do much harm in agreeing with you, and, if you didn't all think alike, it wouldn't matter what I thought, as we've got to be unanimous. I have heard some of the evidence. It's about a murder, isn't it?"

"This is terrible," said the foreman. "What are we to do?"

"Isn't it about a murder?" persisted the inoffensive looking man. "I felt sure it was. And, anyway, I know it is because I read it in the papers."

"Well—that's something," said a juryman. "He has read the papers."

"What was that?" asked the inoffensive looking man.

"You've read the papers," shouted the juryman.

"No," said the inoffensive looking man, "I haven't. I thought we weren't supposed to. But I saw a headline about a murder case. I suppose it is this one. I felt sure it was."

"Well—all we can do is to tell him about it now," said the foreman, "if you agree. I'm hanged if I'm going to tell the judge that one of us hasn't heard anything. He'd eat us alive. D'you all agree to that?"

The suggestion was carried unanimously.

"Now, listen," said the foreman. "We're going to tell you what the evidence is."

"Thank you," said the inoffensive looking man. "I'm very sorry to be a trouble to you."

"Trouble!" said the foreman. "D'you realize a man's life's at stake?"

"I beg your pardon?" said the inoffensive looking man.

"Give me patience," said the foreman. "Now, look, everyone. I can't shout it all at him. I suggest we take it in turns. Suppose we all take a witness and, when one's finished, the others can add anything he's left out. What d'you say to that?"

They said it was about as good as could be expected in the circumstances.

143

"We'd better hurry with lunch and get on with it," said the foreman.

"Would anyone like the horseradish sauce?" said the inoffensive looking man.

They finished their lunch and began to repeat the evidence as best they could, but it soon appeared that they would not have time to complete the process before they were due back in Court again.

"Hadn't we better ask the judge if we can have a little more time?" suggested a juryman. "We can say we're discussing the case. It's perfectly true."

"I don't like the idea much," said the foreman. "The judge will say we ought to wait until we've heard what he has to say."

"I've an idea," said a juryman. "Can't we say that we're considering what counsel for the defence has been saying?"

"About what?"

"About stopping the case."

"How does a jury stop a case?"

"Surely you must have read in the papers sometimes: 'The jury stopped the case.' "

"Yes, I have—certainly, but I'm hanged if I know how they do it. You can't just press a button like on a bus. Does anyone know how it's done?"

"But I don't want to stop the case anyway," said a juryman, who had not intervened in the discussion up to that moment. "I'm interested."

"Interested!" snorted another.

"Yes—and why shouldn't I be? That doesn't mean I shan't give a true verdict according to the evidence. But, if you did what I do all day, you might like a change. Don't often get a chance like this, I can tell you. And I'm not ashamed of saying so."

"Forgive me, gentlemen," said the foreman, " but, at the moment, we only want an excuse for a little more time to tell the evidence to Mr.—Mr.——" and he raised his voice loudly and looked questioningly at the deaf man.

"Greene's my name," said the deaf man, "with three 'e's' if you don't mind."

"You don't pronounce the last 'e', surely?" said a juryman.

"I beg your pardon?" said Mr. Greene.

"Gentlemen, please," said the foreman, "we shall get into trouble if we don't get this settled soon. We only want time to tell Mr. Greene the evidence. We're not trying to stop the case."

"Why not?" said a jurywoman. "If you'll forgive my asking. I write murder stories, as a matter of fact, and I've made the jury stop a case several times."

"You didn't write *Murder on the Village Green* by any chance did you? The jury stopped the case in that."

"Well—I did, as a matter of fact."

"Then you must be April Flower."

"Well—I am, as a matter of fact."

"Is that your real name or a pen name?"

"Well—it's my real name, as a matter of fact."

"Well, this is a bit of all right," said the man who had said he was interested. "I haven't met an author before. May I shake hands with you? This'll last me for the rest of my life."

"Really," said a juryman crossly, "this is no time for small talk. A man's life is at stake."

"If you did what I do all day," said the other, "you'd welcome a little small talk. I shall do my duty just the same as you. But I don't see why I shouldn't get the most out of it."

"I beg your pardon?" said Mr. Greene.

"I wasn't speaking to you, Mr. Greene, but to this other gentleman."

"I didn't quite catch that."

"Mr. Greene," bellowed the foreman, "would you be good enough to listen to me. We haven't time for chatting. We've got to tell you about the case."

"Oh—please do," said Mr. Greene.

"But why shouldn't we stop the case?" said Miss Flower. "We can just say Guilty and then I can go home and write some more stories."

"That's just what you can't do. We haven't heard the defence yet."

"But he's bound to say he didn't do it. We all know that. What's the point of keeping him in suspense? I think it's cruel. At any rate, in *Murder on the Village Green* that's what they did and the judge said it was a very humane thing to do. Then he sentenced him to death. Of course he got off later, but that's another story. It was all a mistake, you know. It was really counsel for the prosecution."

"You wouldn't sign a copy for me, would you?" said the man who was interested.

"Really," said the foreman, "we must get on with the business in hand. We're due back in ten minutes and Mr. Greene doesn't know half the evidence yet. Now, do you agree to my sending a note to the judge asking for another half-hour?"

"Can't do any harm."

"But you're not going to stop the case?" said the man who was interested.

"Of course not, unless we all agree."

"Well, I shan't agree. If you did what I do all day——"

"Very well," cut in the foreman. "We're all agreed then? I'll ring for the usher."

He wrote a note to the judge as follows: "My Lord, the jury would be grateful if they could be allowed a further half-hour to discuss a matter."

Not long afterwards they were summoned into Court.

"The jury have sent me a note, Mr. Pomeroy and Mr. Duffield. They say they want half an hour to discuss something. Have either of you any objection?"

"It's entirely a matter for your Lordship," said Pomeroy.

"Entirely, my Lord," said Duffield, hardly able to conceal his pleasure from his voice. He felt sure that the jury were considering stopping the case. He was really getting somewhere.

"Very well," said the judge. "I can't pretend that I think it's a very good idea to let the jury retire in the middle of a case. But, in all the circumstances, I shall allow them to do so if neither of you objects."

A few minutes later Duffield was speaking to Jill in the corridor outside the Court.

"D'you really mean——" she began, and then burst into tears.

"Now, it isn't over yet," said Duffield. "You must try to keep control of yourself. I know it's difficult. But, you see,

146

you can never tell with a jury. They may stop it and they may not. At any rate, the judge is giving them a chance. He might have refused. It shows he thinks the case isn't too strong. Well, of course, it isn't—but——"

"But what—?"

"Oh—nothing—really——" said Duffield.

"But you must tell me—please—please do. I'm almost bursting, as it is. Don't keep anything from me."

"All right—but you mustn't take too much notice of what I say. I may be wrong. I dare say I often am. In my view, we've got to get Alec off before he goes into the witness box."

"D'you mean he'll be a bad witness?"

"Well—one can't tell. Anyway, there's obviously a real chance that the jury will throw it out. Even if they don't now, they may after I've talked to them a bit more. I shall try to keep going all day to give them the night to think it over."

At that moment the usher came to the Clerk of the Court.

"There's an awful noise going on in the jury room, sir," he said. "They seem to be shouting at one another. Almost as though there were going to be a fight."

"Did you hear what they were saying?"

"Oh, of course not, sir. I was careful to go away so that I couldn't. But I've never heard such a noise from a jury yet. And I've had some experience."

"You don't think anyone's going to get hurt, do you?" said the clerk.

"Well, that's what I was worried about, sir. Shall I go in and see if anything's the matter?"

"Well, you mustn't talk to them, but you might just pop your head in and see if it's all right."

"Very good, sir," said the usher.

He had not exaggerated the noise. The process of one person yelling at Mr. Greene was loud enough, but often some jurymen would disagree with the way the evidence was being put and would intervene loudly. It was no good intervening any other way. Consequently, from time to time the noise sounded like a shouting match. And that's what it was really.

The foreman had just said very loudly: "He threw him over the cliff," and another juryman had immediately followed with:

"Who threw him over the cliff?" and a third: "That's what we're here to find out," when there came a knock at the door, and the usher came in. The noise immediately ceased. He looked round the room, but said nothing.

"Yes?" said the foreman. "Anything you want?"

The usher said nothing, but looked round the room to see if there were any signs of fighting. He found none and, without saying a word, withdrew.

"Well, what's all that in aid of?" said a juryman.

"He's lost something perhaps."

"He might have said what he wanted."

"Well, he didn't. So let's get on. Where had we got to?"

After twenty minutes they had got as far as the evidence of Colonel Brain.

"Colonel Brain said the prisoner admitted his guilt to him."

"He said nothing of the kind. He made it quite clear that they just had a joke together. Don't you remember him laughing in the witness box? The judge had to stop him in the end."

"Funny how infectious laughter is. He had the whole Court laughing."

"Who was laughing?" said Mr. Greene.

"The whole Court."

"What's that got to do with it?"

"Nothing, but the point is," shouted a juryman, "that there wasn't any real admission. It was just a joke. Colonel Brain said so himself."

"That was why he laughed then?" said Mr. Greene. "At the recollection of the joke?"

"Absolutely," shouted the juryman.

"I'm not so sure that it was a joke," said the foreman.

"Well, you laughed anyway," said the man who was interested.

"I was laughing because I couldn't help it. Everybody was."

"I don't think we should laugh at a murder trial."

"I agree, but we couldn't help it. It was infectious. I could see the judge had a struggle himself."

"I don't see how you can convict a man just because he made a joke. It wouldn't be safe anyway."

"What other evidence is there?" asked Mr. Greene.

"What more d'you want?" said a juryman. "He threw him over the cliff. If that isn't murder, I don't know what is."

"You mean someone threw him over the cliff. There's no evidence that it was the prisoner."

"Then why is he in the dock? He wouldn't be there unless he'd thrown him over."

"You're implying that everyone who stands in the dock is guilty."

"Well, they are mostly, aren't they? The police don't charge people unless they're satisfied they're guilty."

"Really!" said a juryman indignantly. "There doesn't seem much object in having a judge or jury if that's the right point of view. Just chop their heads off and be done with it."

"There's no need to be offensive."

"I'm not being in the least offensive, but to hear someone who's sworn to try a case well and truly express the view that there's really nothing to try is rather alarming. This isn't a police state, you know."

"I never said it was. I only implied that the police don't prosecute unless they're sure a man's guilty."

"That doesn't mean the police are right."

"Please, gentlemen," said the foreman, "we've a lot to do. Could you reserve this discussion till we're considering our verdict? All we're doing now is telling Mr. Greene the evidence."

While the jury were thus engaged, Kingsdown thought it might give him an opportunity to mention the matter of Mr. Low again. This time he was more successful.

"My Lord," he said, "I should not have ventured to mention this matter to your Lordship but for the later evidence given by Colonel Brain, the witness to whom my client spoke. My Lord, I do not, nor does my client, wish in any way to minimize the seriousness of the offence of interfering with a witness, but I do most respectfully submit to your Lordship that when a person hears a witness give evidence which he knows to be wrong, he may be, to some extent, excused for trying to persuade him to be accurate. Of course, he ought not to interfere with him, but I do suggest that his behaviour is not morally blameworthy."

"How did your client know that Colonel Brain's evidence was wrong?" asked the judge.

"Because he had spoken to him, my Lord. If your Lordship would allow my client to give evidence, he has been brought from prison and is available."

"Very well," said the judge. "Undoubtedly Colonel Brain is an unusual type of witness. I will hear what your client has to say."

Mr. Low was accordingly brought into court and went into the witness box. A warder sat behind him.

"Well," said the judge, "what d'you want to say about this?"

"First, my Lord," said Mr. Low, "I would like to offer to your Lordship my very humble apologies for doing something which I realize was wrong, though I do assure your Lordship my object was only to persuade the witness to tell the truth."

"You say that your object was in furtherance of justice?" said the judge.

"To try to persuade the witness to tell the truth," repeated Mr. Low.

"That's the same thing," said the judge.

"If your Lordship pleases," said Mr. Low. "Now, my Lord, I have known Colonel Brain for some time and I am aware that his mind does not work quite as everyone else's mind works."

"I can agree with you there," said the judge.

"Well, my Lord, Colonel Brain having told me that he had had a jocular conversation with the prisoner about the man who killed Gilbert Essex, I was astounded when I heard him say in all seriousness that the accused had in effect admitted his guilt to him. So I felt that I ought to try to remind him of what had really happened, the charge being such a serious one. But, as I said before, my Lord, I now realize the gravity of doing such a thing and I promise I will never do such a thing again."

"Well," said the judge, "unless Colonel Brain was tampered with overnight, he did unquestionably give a very different account of his interview with the prisoner in cross-examination from what he said in examination-in-chief. And it is true to say that he swore he had spoken to no one about the case. Personally I am prepared to accept that. He was not the easiest of witnesses, but he did not appear to me to be untruthful. In these circumstances, it seems to me that I can take a more lenient view of your behaviour than I thought possible before. In all the circumstances, I am prepared to order your immediate release."

"I am most grateful to your Lordship," said Mr. Low.

"I am very much obliged, my Lord," said Mr. Kingsdown.

"Very well then, I will rise now until the jury is ready."

"I think," said Mr. Low to Elizabeth as soon as they were reunited, "that we ought to have a cup of coffee to celebrate. The stuff in prison was undrinkable."

"I'll stand you a cup," said Elizabeth, "but there'll be no celebration until these wretched young people are out of their mess."

"How's it going?"

"Well, it could be worse. I think we neutralized old Brain all right, but whether the jury will stop the case is another matter. They're apparently talking it over now."

"Well," said Mr. Low, "I think you've done very well. If all goes according to plan, I'll get you a new hat."

"I'd much prefer a promise."

"Of what?"

"That you won't go interfering in other people's affairs any more."

"We'll see," said Mr. Low. "If this comes off, it will have been worth it."

"And if it doesn't—?"

"I'll be in the same boat as Morland."

"How d'you mean?"

"Well, he killed a man with the best possible motives, and I shall have done the same."

"Yes—but you won't be hanged and he will be. Hardly the same boat."

"Well, there is that. But thinking of it won't make it any better. Let's have some more coffee and hope. There's nothing else we can do."

Meanwhile, in the jury room the last piece of evidence had been shouted at Mr. Greene.

"Just in time," said the foreman. "I'll ring for the usher."

CHAPTER XVI

THE VERDICT OF YOU ALL?

"BUT, just a moment," said Mr. Greene. "Is that all?"

"Yes—as far as we can remember."

"But I don't understand," said Mr. Greene. "I thought the prisoner was charged with murder. I haven't heard any evidence that he did it yet. Perhaps I missed something."

"Well—if you did," shouted the foreman, "it wasn't our fault. We've all shouted till we're hoarse."

"You haven't told me what counsel's been saying."

"He's been telling us to stop the case," said the man who was interested. "But I want to hear some more."

"Telling us to drop the case?"

"STOP the case," shouted the man who was interested.

"All right," said Mr. Greene, "I agree."

"But I don't."

"I beg your pardon?"

"I DON'T."

"Why not? Even I know they've got to prove the case. And, if they haven't, that's an end of it, surely. Or do you think they have proved it?"

"No, I wouldn't say that," said the man who was interested, "but I'd like to hear what the prisoner has to say. I've never heard one before."

"But surely," said Miss Flower, "if they haven't proved the case and you've sworn to try it according to the evidence, you just have to say Not Guilty."

"I thought you wanted to say Guilty."

"Well, that was before I'd thought about it properly. But, listening to everything that was told to Mr. Greene, it didn't seem to come to very much. It came to much more than that in *Murder on the Village Green*. Blood was found on him and all that."

"I never heard that part," said Mr. Greene. "Who said blood was found on him?"

"No one. That's just in a book."

At that moment the usher came in. " Are you ready?" he asked.

A few minutes later the jury were back in Court. Everyone waited expectantly for the foreman to say something. Even the judge looked at them for a moment, but, as the foreman remained seated and did not appear to want to say anything, he turned his head towards counsel's seats and said: "Very well, Mr. Duffield, you had better continue."

Very disappointed that he had not yet succeeded in persuading the jury to stop the case, Duffield was nevertheless determined to make a final effort and to keep his opening address going until the adjournment. He also decided not to indicate by one word what his defence was going to be. Had he done so and had the jury then tried to stop the case, the judge might have intervened and invited them to hear what Duffield had said proved by evidence. But, provided he contented himself with referring to the evidence for the prosecution, the judge could make no such suggestion. It was a formidable task to talk to the jury for two hours on a subject he had already dealt with pretty thoroughly. "But I can't help it," he said to himself, "if I bore them or even if the judge gets fed up and interrupts me. I must keep going until the adjournment so as to give them an opportunity to think about it overnight. It's our only chance."

He looked along the two lines of the jury, trying to see if he could single out either one of the jury who was standing out against him or one of them who would carry on his advocacy for him in the jury room. It is not unusual for counsel to select, and make his speech, to a juryman who looks intelligent, attentive, and likely to carry weight with the remainder of the jury when they are considering their verdict. But, of course, counsel may make a mistake in his selection. Even the most experienced counsel can do this. As did Duffield in this case.

Looking carefully at each of the jury before he began, he decided to choose Mr. Greene. Mr. Greene soon became aware that counsel was talking at him and did his best to hear and lip read, but with little success. But his efforts made him appear so particularly attentive that Duffield felt sure he had made a good choice. He would have been horrified to learn that Mr. Greene only caught a word here and there. After he had gone on for half an hour, the judge began to get restive. After three-quarters of an hour he interrupted: "Forgive me, Mr. Duffield," he said, "but is all this really necessary? You have another speech, you know, later."

"I hope it won't be necessary, my Lord."

"I dare say you do, but if you think that repeating yourself time and again will be less likely to make it necessary, I can only say that I disagree with you. The jury aren't fools, you know."

"I quite follow what's in your Lordship's mind," said Duffield, "but, unless your Lordship says I must not do so, I propose to devote the remainder of the afternoon to my opening."

"The remainder of the afternoon, Mr. Duffield?"

"Yes, my Lord—unless, of course, the jury make this unnecessary."

"Mr. Duffield, I really must ask you to refrain from making that kind of remark."

"Surely, my Lord, I am entitled to ask the jury to stop the case?"

"You have already done so—not once but several times and the jury have apparently decided not to do so. Your right now is to open your case."

"If your Lordship pleases. With your Lordship's leave, I will continue."

And Duffield, looking hard at Mr. Greene, began again. Mr. Greene had relaxed during the dialogue between the judge and counsel, but he soon became conscious that he was being talked at and sat stiff and uncomfortable and trying to look intelligent for the remainder of the afternoon. The rest of the jury started to get restless, even the man who was interested, regretting, if ever so slightly, that they hadn't stopped the case and gone away. Duffield was certainly becoming a bore. But the man who was interested comforted himself with the thought that there was the prisoner to come, and he bore the ordeal as manfully as he could. At five o'clock the judge intervened: "Will you be much longer, Mr. Duffield?"

"Not more than an hour or so, my Lord."

"Really," said the judge. "There must be some limit to this. I shall have to consider whether I can allow you to go on in the morning. Perhaps you will consider, too, over the adjournment, whether it's likely to help your client much."

The Court adjourned.

As Mr. Low and Elizabeth left the court, Jill came up to them.

"I'm so sorry to trouble you," she said unhappily, "but—but could you——" but Mr. Low interrupted before she could finish.

"Can I tell you what will happen tomorrow?" he said. "Yes, I can. Your husband will be acquitted and you and he will live happily ever after. Provided, of course, he doesn't do it again."

"D'you mean that?" said Jill.

"Of course I do. Dry your eyes and have a good night. It'll be all right tomorrow. You'll see."

Jill tried to thank him, but could not, and went hurriedly away to burst into tears of relief.

"That was very wrong of you, Ambrose," said Elizabeth, when Jill was out of earshot. "You can't possibly know what'll happen tomorrow and, if things go wrong, the poor girl will be distracted."

"So she will," said her husband, "but, if things go wrong, she'd be distracted in any event. The shock will be just as great whatever I said. All I'm doing is to give her a better night and plenty of hope. There can't be much wrong with that. If he does go down, it won't be any worse for her because of what I've said. Nothing anybody said could make it worse. She'll be at the end of everything. Indeed, she might be able to work up a little anger against me. Which would be a good thing. So, if I'm wrong, I've done no harm and, if I'm right, I've done some good. Agreed?"

"You're right as usual, I suppose," said Elizabeth, "but I'll wring your neck if he doesn't get off. It'll all be your fault."

"We've had all this out before. I've only made one mistake in this case. I've arranged the evidence so that any normal man ought to be able to get off. I produced enough evidence to get him committed for trial and not enough to convict him. I must say you did well with the old colonel. I was a bit worried about him. But you see he turned up trumps in the end. Thanks to you, I'll agree."

"Then what's the mistake?"

"Well, it's obvious Duffield's terrified of putting him in the witness box. He'll have to, of course, if the jury don't stop the case, but he obviously thinks he'll be a bad witness. That's my error of judgment. I didn't give him credit for being such a bad liar."

"Judging him by yourself, I suppose."

"Right as always, my sweet."

Meanwhile, the man who was interested was on his way home in an omnibus.

"Wonder what they'll do," said the man next to him, who was looking at a paper. "Why did the jury have a confab, d'you think?"

"I'm on the jury," said the man who was interested, "and I can't tell you."

"On the jury? That must be exciting."

"Just a matter of doing one's duty, old man. That's the way I look at it."

"But you must get a thrill out of being there all the time and seeing everything—the judge and lawyers and witnesses, and having a man's life in your hands."

"That's not the way I look at it. Have you ever had a man's life in your hands?"

"Can't say that I have."

"Well—wait till you have, old man, before you talk of it being exciting."

"Sorry—no offence, I hope."

"No offence, old man, but some people don't realize what a strain it is on the jury, that's all."

He got out at the next stop and soon reached his home. He

let himself in, took off his coat, and went into the sitting-room. He was happily married, but his wife and he were not demonstratively affectionate.

"Hullo, Liz," he said.

"Hullo, Bert. You back?"

"Yes," he said and flopped into the armchair.

"How many times have I got to tell you about those springs?" said his wife. "Might as well have an elephant sitting on them."

"If you did what I do all day——" began her husband.

"I know, I know," said his wife. "If I did what you do all day, I'd want to sit down with a flop. Well, for one thing, I shouldn't, and for another thing, you haven't been doing it all day. You've been sitting nice and comfortably listening to a case. How's it going, by the way?"

"Can't tell you the secrets of the jury room."

"Did I ask you to? I can see in the paper, if I want to."

"Well, as a matter of fact, but don't let it go any further, it's eleven to one at the moment. And I'm the one. The others want to stop the case and let him off."

"And you want to convict him."

"I wouldn't say that, but it's another thing to stop the case in the middle."

"Well, you stick to your principles," said his wife. "Don't you give way to clamour."

"Have you ever known me?" he said. They both laughed.

"That counsel of his," he went on, "he doesn't give way either. He goes on for ever. Says he'll be another hour. Said the same thing I don't know how many times. Might be paid by the word."

"P'raps he is."

"Never thought of that. I suppose he is, in a way. He must get more the longer it lasts. But he looks a decent chap. Shouldn't think that was his reason. But he is a bore! Wonder if he's married. Sorry for his wife if he repeats himself as often at home. Now, if he did what——"

"I know," said his wife. "He repeats himself."

The next morning the jury were in their places some ten minutes before the judge arrived. They took the opportunity of having a whispered conversation. As soon as the judge had entered and the case had been called, Duffield got up to continue his speech. The judge looked at him and began to speak. In consequence, neither of them noticed that the foreman had stood up too.

"Mr. Duffield," said the judge, "I've been considering this matter overnight. Although naturally substantial licence is allowed to counsel for the defence, there must come a time when I have the right to intervene. Otherwise theoretically you might go on talking for ever."

At that moment Duffield felt his gown pulled by his next-door neighbour, who pointed out the foreman to him.

"My Lord," said Duffield, "the foreman of the jury appears to want to address your Lordship."

The judge turned his head.

"Yes, Mr. Foreman?" he said. "Do you want to say something?"

"My Lord," said the foreman, "the jury would like to stop the case, with your Lordship's permission, and find the prisoner Guilty."

"Mr. Foreman," began the judge sternly. He was about to tell the jury that they were acting in a most improper way and to say that the trial could not possibly go on before such an unfair set of people, and that there would have to be a new trial.

"I mean Not Guilty," said the foreman.

"Well—which do you mean?" said the judge.

"Oh—Not Guilty, my Lord. I got a little confused. I haven't done this before, I'm afraid, and I was a little tensed up."

"I see," said the judge. "Well—we'd better make quite certain."

The judge spoke to the clerk, who then addressed the jury.

"Members of the jury," he said, "are you agreed upon your verdict?"

"We are."

"Do you find the prisoner Alec Morland Not Guilty and is that the verdict of you all?"

"We do and it is." said the foreman.

"You are discharged," said the judge to Alec.

The cheering which threatened to break out in the court was sternly suppressed, and: "Call the next case," said the judge.

Soon, in the corridor outside the court, there was a confused mass of people all trying to shake hands with Alec and Jill. After a short time, the police managed to make a path for them to leave the Assize Court. Elizabeth put her car at their disposal and they drove away amid considerable cheering.

"Well," said Mr. Low to Elizabeth, "will you and Master Low mind a walk?"

"Miss Low and I," said Elizabeth, "would enjoy one. And might I add that, if anything else had happened, she would have been early for her appointment. I think we'd like a drink."

They went to the nearest hotel.

"Don't you ever do such a thing again," said Elizabeth, after her first Dry Martini. "Promise?"

"But I don't keep them, my sweet," said Mr. Low sadly. "We'll just have to hope that the next one's easier. And anyway," he added, "you must admit that we've made two people gloriously happy."

"Five," said Elizabeth.

Just as Colonel Brain was leaving the Assize Court, Bobbie rushed up to him.

"Hullo, my boy," said the colonel. "What are you so excited about?"

"Oh—Colonel," said Bobbie, "I can't thank you enough."

"Thank me? What for, my boy?"

"For your help. I'm engaged."

"But we haven't written the letter yet, my boy—not quite, anyway." The colonel paused for a moment. "You haven't been trying my direct assault method, I suppose? Hug 'em and hope."

"That's exactly what I have done, Colonel."

"There you are, you see, my boy. I thought you told me she wouldn't stand for it."

"Oh—she wouldn't have," said Bobbie. "Not Alison. I tried it on Agatha, I'm afraid. And I'm so happy. Of course we can't be married for years. She's younger than I am. But it's just marvellous. I can't thank you enough, Colonel. I should never have done it but for you."

"Well—that's all right, my boy, glad to have been of help. Now you won't have to go pig-sticking after all. Or was that someone else?"

Back at their home Alec and Jill could hardly believe their good fortune. After she had recovered some composure, Jill said:

"It really is you, isn't it? And you're free and we're safe for ever. Will I wake up suddenly? Tell me it's true."

"It's true, my darling," he said, and kissed her. "We'll have to send the Lows something for Christmas," he added. "I think that'll be the nicest way to thank them. What a clever girl you were to go and see them."

"I didn't think so at one time."

"Nor did I—I confess—but the proof of the pudding's in the eating and it tastes awful good to me," and he kissed her again.

Laura Duffield had heard the news and greeted her husband on the doorstep.

"Well done," she said. "We must go out and celebrate."

"Can't, I'm afraid, darling. Got too much to do. We'll have to save it up till the vac. This case has put all my paper work back. I'll be up most of the night."

"Why—oh—why did I marry a barrister?" she said.

"Because I asked you," he said. "You can sit on my knee for ten minutes."

Which is about all a busy member of the Bar has time for.

The man who was interested reached home an hour after the verdict.

"You're back early," said his wife. "How come?"

"We stopped the case."

"I thought you wouldn't agree."

"Well—I thought it over on the way to court—and, as it was eleven to one against me and he was bound to get off in the end anyway, I thought I'd give in." He hesitated, and then said:

"Besides, between you and me, I rather wanted to get back to my job."